PAT BURDEN

Bury Him Kindly

THE CRIME CLUB
An Imprint of HarperCollins *Publishers*

First published in Great Britain in 1991
by The Crime Club, an imprint of
HarperCollins Publishers, 77–85 Fulham Palace Road,
Hammersmith, London W6 8JB

British Library Cataloguing in Publication Data

Burden, Pat
  Bury him kindly.
  I. Title
  823.914[F]

ISBN 0 00 232344 3

Photoset in Linotron Baskerville by
Rowland Phototypesetting Ltd
Bury St Edmunds, Suffolk
Printed and bound in Great Britain by
HarperCollins Book Manufacturing, Glasgow

CHAPTER 1

Police Sergeant Andy Miller drew up behind the Range-Rover and ancient Morris Minor parked on a grassy verge some yards from Keeper's Cottage, and strode to the garden gate.

He walked in to sounds of merriment. 'Having yourselves a party?' He grinned, raised his voice a notch. 'Can anybody join in?'

The long sloping lawn was littered with men and dogs, all of them scanning the woodland which surrounded the cottage beyond wire fencing. Andy recognized two of the faces immediately: Tod Arkwright, retired gamekeeper and local gloom-and-doom merchant, as miserable as sin to look at yet frequently the life and soul, as they say; and big, bearded Jack Carter, also known as Jack the Poacher, a pseudonym he applied to his country books and articles, sporting a guernsey which made him look more like a deep-sea fisherman than a writer; but then Jack hadn't always been a writer. The duffel coat? The wearer turned his head. Of course. Reverend William Brewerton, Vicar of Oakleigh, and owner of the Morris Minor. He should have known: these four were frequently together. The fourth was Bassett, ex-Detective Chief Superintendent Henry Bassett, whose cottage this was.

It was Bassett who came to greet Andy as the young sergeant stepped inside the gate, calling to the others, 'Police, you lot! Come to tell us we're making too much noise!'

'Less of the you lot!'

It was Tod who informed Andy, one of the few coppers he could get along with—Andy occasionally bought him a pint at the village pub—that only minutes before all hell had been let loose among Bassett's chickens. 'Vixen,' Tod rumbled lugubriously. 'Daylight raider a-chancing her luck. Cubs to feed, I suppose. Ar.'

Jack joined them, ginger terrier at his heels. 'Probably just spotted her.' He pointed to Gert and Daisy, two inseparable brown hens perched on a low branch of a hefty though gnarled old cherry tree. 'They are the culprits. Won't stop in.'

'True,' Bassett told Andy. 'Go for a daily walkabout. Probably lead the vixen here, teasing the animal unmercifully, then have the cheek to fly up there and sound the alarm.'

'Varmints,' Andy opined, grinning.

Jack echoed Tod's warning that once a fox had chooks marked it would get them; unless Bassett penned the hens in during the day as well as night he was doomed to lose the lot.

'Would foxes scale the fence?' Andy asked.

'Put it this way,' Tod said. 'They'll be a-practising.'

Peace resumed. 'What's he a-doing?' Tod rumbled, referring to Willy Brewerton, who had halted on his trek up the garden to meet them and was staring at something out of their view. 'Willy!' he called, as in a body he and the others moved across the lawn to join the Vicar. 'We've brung you another sinner! The police sergeant here—'

Tod didn't finish. Reverend Willy turned his head, a bemused expression on his kindly face. 'I was just watching Cocky there—' Bassett's prized rooster down in the bottom garden, all spurs, proud chest and high tail feathers normally; at this moment tail-less and looking half-plucked, in fact downright bedraggled.

Gamekeeper Tod broke the ensuing silence. 'He's a-strutting round like Liberace—and he's got his backside out of his trousers!'

The grinning Andy took this as his cue to leave. They would have fences to fix; for him duty beckoned.

'I'm actually on my way to Bletch Heath, car there, believed to be abandoned. Yellow Datsun. Ring a bell? The chap who reported it thinks it's been there three days; but if it belongs to a known walker, bird-watcher . . . ? No . . . ?' Andy shrugged when they all shook their heads. 'Not to worry. Just a thought. Don't want to go making a fuss if it belongs to someone who's simply communing with nature. It's not exactly a beauty-spot area, but there are woods there.'

'Ar. There are woods there,' Tod rumbled darkly after Andy had gone, for the young sergeant had described where the Datsun was. 'Robby Meddlar's territory. Ar. And I've been a-hearing a few things.'

'What things?' Jack inquired, as they trooped in the direction of the cottage door. It was time for some refreshment, the fencing could wait a while.

'Never you mind,' Tod replied.

The dogs, a mixture of breeds like their owners, had already made a beeline for Bassett's hearthrug, big enough to accommodate all of them: no fire in the grate, this was April and the weather was sunny and mild, but dogs are creatures of habit. So also are men. Presently stockinged feet joined the dogs round a bare fireplace, mugs of steaming tea and rolls of cheese and chutney much in evidence.

'What things?' bearded Jack repeated, lowering himself into an armchair. He lived nearer to Bletch Heath than did Tod and Reverend Willy. He'd heard of Alice Meddlar and Robby, believed he'd bumped into Robby on one occasion. They had surprised each other, coming face to face across a line of blackberry bushes. The man had frozen, and before Jack had time to do more than utter an hello, had turned and disappeared like a creature of the wild, fearful of predators. Jack had looked out for the man since, he had looked so lonely. He had never spotted him, yet often he had known somehow that the man was there. Somewhere.

'Things,' Tod said. He drank from his mug, wiped his

mouth, peered accusingly at Jack the Poacher. 'You must've heard a few yerself, you've been back more'n six years now. I know it's round there and the rest o' the Malverns you do your a-naturing bit and Bletch Heath's off your track, but you must've heard things, must've.'

'I haven't,' Reverend Willy said. 'Who is he, this Robby Meddlar? Do I know him?'

'No, you won't be a-knowing him, Willy. Reclused, him and his mother. Never see 'em one year's end to the next. And there's them as are a-saying it's just as well.'

'Oh?' Reverend Willy's baby-smooth forehead took on a frown. He was particularly interested because the tiny village of Bletch Heath, six miles away, was soon to become one of his parishes.

Tod shuffled his feet, ignored the gentle probe. 'Runs like a scared rabbit if you gets near. Runs fast enough to meet hisself a-coming back. Ar, the man's a Simony.'

'A Simony?'

'A Simon.'

'A simpleton,' Jack said quietly.

Reverend Willy Brewerton nodded, as if that explained everything. 'Then I must call on them,' he said cheerfully.

'It'll be your first call and your last.' Tod's long lugubrious chin grew longer. He turned oval eyes on Willy, studied him in silence until the Vicar met his gaze. Then: 'You'll end up a-looking like Cocky. Turn her shotgun on you, she will, his mother, Alice. Her'll give your backside a good old peppering.'

'Oh dear!' Willy's face fell.

'With rock salt,' Jack qualified. 'Stings!' he added comically.

It was fun talk, none of it meant to be taken too seriously. On the face of it, that is. But Bassett had been watching Jack and it seemed to him that the grin which spread underneath the beard was just a little tight. He sensed an underlying tension.

CHAPTER 2

That evening Bassett was sitting cosily in the room he called his parlour, in his large leather wrap-around armchair— the one his late wife, Mary, used fondly to refer to as his security blanket. He had a book in one hand, a nightcap whisky in the other, and pup, his golden labrador, snored contentedly across his feet. In short, Bassett was enjoying what to him constituted one of life's pleasures: perfect peace.

Suddenly pup shot up on to all four legs, hackles raised, and gave out an enormous bark. Bassett's whisky shot out of the glass, the book fell from his fingers, and his hair stood on end.

'I wish you wouldn't do that!' he scolded the dog.

It was Jack at the door, his footsteps down the path so soft that only the dog had heard them. 'Frightened the life out of me!' Bassett said, letting his friend in.

'Haven't knocked yet.' But Jack's tone commiserated, albeit he chuckled; he'd heard the bark, and he had dogs of his own. 'Hope you don't mind my bothering you at this hour, Harry. I've brought a bottle to oil my welcome. Like to have a word before things get out of hand.'

A few minutes later, pup now across his feet, Jack said, 'Remember the Smiths? Daniel and Fleur?'

Bassett nodded. 'Settled gipsies. Smallholding on the road to Ross.'

'Stolen porcelain, the death of an old lady. Aaron and Isaac, whose innocence you proved.'

'You did most of the work, Jack, as I recall.'

Jack's beard twitched modestly. 'To get to the point: Alice Meddlar is Fleur Smith's distant cousin by marriage.'

'Small world.'

Jack smiled. 'I didn't know myself until old Daniel Smith came to see me late this afternoon.'

'So. Alice Meddlar. Simpleton son. Abandoned car. You've come to tell me there's a connection.'

'Might be,' Jack said. 'Daniel has a nasty feeling they could be in trouble.'

'Go on,' Bassett said. 'I'm listening.'

'There's not much gipsy in Alice's blood—I did say they were distantly related. Apparently she worked as a lady's maid at Bletch House before and during the war. Married from there, moved away, returned twenty-five years ago, bought a place called Tree Tops—and there she and Robby have lived like hermits ever since.

'None of the Smiths saw much of her for the first fifteen years; when she cut herself off from society she shut the door on the family as well. But about ten years ago—that very bad winter we had, 1981 wasn't it?—Daniel got to worrying about her, went to see her, found her a shade more friendly, and now visits her a couple of times a year. Brief visits—Hello, how are you? Bones a-creaking but otherwise all right. Oh good, I'll say cheerio, then. That kind of thing. As you know, Daniel is settled but his family are still tribal. He was duty bound once she had accepted him again to keep an eye on her.

'He was on his way to see her today, to take her some flowers for her birthday—passed the lay-by Andy Miller told us about, saw the police searching a car, and so carried straight on. Occurred to him that the car might be stolen, he's no affection for the police after the Aaron and Isaac affair, and so he preferred to be out of the vicinity when they began asking questions.

'Anyhow, he drove on, fetching up eventually at Bletch Heath village shop. A 15-cwt van pulled in behind him. Turned out to be the shopkeeper, who started telling his wife and a couple of customers about this car found abandoned in Cooper's Lane, been there three days. As Daniel told it, the shopkeeper must have arrived at the lay-by after he did because the police were taping the area off, and had stopped the shopkeeper to ask him if the car was familiar. Known nature-lover, et cetera, same as Andy Miller asked us.

'When the shopkeeper got to describing the car—a yellow Datsun—one of the customers, a woman, went into a tizzy. The car sounded like Eileen's, she said; she hoped nothing had happened to her, that lay-by was next door to the Meddlar place—and she'd heard that Alice Meddlar ran strangers off her property at the end of a shotgun. She went haring off, white as a sheet, muttering something about having warned Olivia not to interfere.

'Daniel was all ears. He's never broadcast his relationship to Alice, and Alice never would have, so conversations in the shop carried on around him. No one actually *knew*, but there was a general feeling among them, apparently, that a—a Mrs Mulholland, he thinks the name was—that somebody, at any rate, was keen to have a welfare officer friend to see Robby, perhaps Eileen was that friend.'

Initially Daniel hadn't taken any of this to heart, Jack said. Gossip, surmise, were some folks' bedfellows. Lots of yellow cars around, the one on the lay-by was probably nothing like Eileen's, they had all been jumping to conclusions.

'But he dropped in at the pub in Bletch Heath at tea-time, Harry. Was going to have a snack meal before having another crack at getting to Alice's. He overheard them talking in the pub. About police searching hedges and ditches in Cooper's Lane—for a body obviously, was the consensus. Robby was mentioned. Somebody called him a mad bugger. Worried the life out of Daniel. Not everyone was out to get Robby, but there were a couple of men—one in particular—who had real lynch-mob mentalities. They made it pretty clear—or rather, clear to Daniel from the way they spoke—that if the Datsun did belong to this

Eileen, and if anything *had* happened to her, they'd make
sure the police knew where to look—'

Bassett interrupted. 'Have the Meddlars ever given
trouble in the past? Frightened children, or—?'

Jack shook his head. 'Shouldn't think so. Be one of the
first subjects aired, wouldn't it? According to Daniel, there
was none of that.'

'So why the animosity now?'

'Exactly,' Jack replied. 'Daniel has been asking himself
the same question. Granted, Alice and Robby do have a
certain reputation. They're odd. Both of them. Alice did, in
the past, pepper a backside or two. Or it might even have
been just the once, and word spread and stuck. She might
simply have threatened, and the rest can be put down to
jokers and fertile imaginations. It's true, Robby never leaves
his patch, never meets people, runs away when he's approached; but for twenty-five years the village has accepted
them for what they are. Now—suddenly—they are mad.
Why? What happened?'

Jack paused while pup switched loyalties. When she
was draped once more at Bassett's feet he continued,
'Daniel mulled over everything he overheard and put
two and two together. A newcomer to Bletch Heath—
this Mrs Mulholland—with up-to-date ideas on mental
welfare, wants to take Robby out of seclusion and into
society; at least into some Centre where he could mix
with people of his own kind . . . Problem, Harry. Alice
would've been dead set against the idea. It's been
suggested in the past, by Fleur for one. Alice always
jumped down their throats, she can't get Victorian
institutions out of her head. No son of hers is going into
one of those places! Anyone tries . . . !

'All bluff.' Jack spread his hands. 'Empty threats, Daniel
assured me. But he thinks she may have voiced them to
other people. Apparently she has groceries delivered now.
She's friendly with some girl. He's afraid that if she's

sounded off in front of them—' Jack's massive shoulders moved expressively.

A moment, and Bassett asked, 'How old is Robby?'

'In his thirties. Born to Alice late in life. She is nearing eighty.'

'What do they live on?' No sooner uttered than cancelled, by Bassett answering himself. 'Daniel Smith and the family would have looked after them.'

'Matter of fact, that wasn't necessary,' Jack said. 'Alice is wealthy in her own right. Her husband left her well provided for.'

'He's dead?'

A nod: Yes.

'This shotgun business,' Bassett said. 'Does Alice still own a shotgun, would you know?'

'As a deterrent. To wave at louts, tearaways, and would-be burglars and tormentors.'

'Do you know them, either of them? You know every inch of these hills. Have you ever spoken to them?'

'Until I was told about the grocery delivery and the girl Alice is reputedly friendly with I would have said nobody knew them, Harry. I'd heard of them, a pair of harmless eccentrics who want to be left alone.'

'You wouldn't know, then, if they used a shotgun for shooting rabits, pigeons, pheasants.'

'According to Daniel, they kill nothing. Bit like you.' Jack grinned. 'Hens for laying, not for eating; and in winter food and water put out for foxes and all.'

'Hmm. Righto!' Bassett eased slippered feet out gently from under a sleeping pup, and stood up. 'I'll make a telephone call, find out what's going on.'

Jack got up too. 'You know what's really worrying Daniel? What will happen if and when the police turn up to question Alice and Robby. Tod had it bang on: the man runs. Even from Daniel. Have coppers knocking on the door and Robby hides—which he will—he's likely to end up in a cell with the key thrown away. It would destroy his mother.'

'Wouldn't do Robby any favours either,' Bassett said. 'Especially if the poor bloke's innocent.'

The telephone was in the hall. Jack in tow, Bassett dialled the number of Glevebourne Police Station, asked to speak to Inspector Bob Greenaway.

Bob wasn't there. Not surprising. It was late now, and even coppers have to sleep.

'Perhaps you can help me, Tom.' Bassett was on speaking terms with the duty sergeant. 'This Datsun at Bletch Heath: I made a note of the registered owner's name but appear to have mislaid the blessed thing.'

The duty sergeant was well aware that ex-Detective Chief Superintendent Bassett occasionally worked in an unofficial capacity with Bob Greenaway. 'I can get it for you,' he said with some deference. 'Ring you back?'

'Good of you, Tom. Search still in progress?'

It wasn't; would resume at first light.

Ergo no body yet. Bassett passed on the information to Jack. Then: 'While we're waiting, anything else you can tell me about Robby Meddlar? Plain curiosity. An occupational hazard,' Bassett said happily.

Jack's mood matched his. 'Same here. I asked old Daniel a few questions but there wasn't much to tell. Robby's in his thirties, works hard around the house and grounds. Fetches wood for the fires. Daniel's only seen him once close-to in the past ten years. As I said, he runs and hides.'

'Even from Daniel?'

'Even from Daniel,' Jack said.

'Any idea whether Robby was within earshot when they spoke to his mother about a Centre or whatever?'

Jack's reply was a shrug: Sorry.

'So you don't know what his reaction would have been. But anyhow he runs and hides,' Bassett mused aloud. He looked intently at Jack. 'From everybody? Grocery man?

The girl his mother is friendly with? Presumably then he would also have run from Eileen.' Jack said that as he understood it Robby *met* no one. On a slightly different tack: 'Does he *ever* leave his patch?'

'By all accounts, no. They have a fair amount of land, and there are woods adjoining. No public paths, so he has the woods more or less to himself.'

'Robby's territory, as Tod said.' Bassett flicked an eyebrow. 'He is known mainly by reputation, then. Am I right? Imagined or otherwise. Alice Meddlar and her shotgun. Robby and—?' Eyebrow arched.

'You'd have to say Robby and his woodcutting tools.'

Bassett murmured lazily, 'Robby and his woodcutting tools.' Was jolted. Altered his voice. 'Oh lord.'

The telephone rang. Good news for Jack.

'Daniel can sleep easily tonight,' Bassett told him. 'The car isn't Eileen's, whoever she is; it's registered to a Mr Philip Read.'

Jack's relief showed. 'Philip Read. Good. I'll let Daniel know. He'll be grateful.' A fat wink conveyed his own personal thank-you. 'Let's hope they find him alive and well.'

They shook hands at the gate. Bassett watched until the tail lights of Jack's Range-Rover disappeared into darkness along the unlit lane; and decided that he was right to have withheld that additional piece of information at this stage.

What he hadn't told Jack was that Philip Read was believed to work for a social services department.

Likewise, Bassett had thought better of voicing the question: How might Robby Meddlar have reacted if he couldn't run, if indeed he was *cornered*?

CHAPTER 3

It was barely dawn. A persistent telephone woke Bassett from sweet slumber. The voice at the other end of the line was female, educated, not young; agitated.

'Mr Bassett? . . . My name is Annette Gray. You don't know me, and it's dreadfully early, I know, but I wanted to be sure and catch you. I do apologize, but—' She took a breath; began again. 'I live in Bletch Heath. Your cleaning lady, Sally? Her son John is one of my neighbours. He suggested that I speak to you, he was sure you wouldn't mind.'

'Don't mind at all—er—is it Mrs Gray?'

'Mrs Gray, yes.' She rushed on. 'May I ask you—do you know anything about a car found at Bletch Heath? Is it a yellow Datsun?'

'I believe so.'

'And is it true that the police are looking for a body?'

'Not exactly,' Bassett said wisely. 'They are looking for the driver, who may be missing.'

'Missing. Oh dear.' A low moan came from Annette Gray, 'missing' and 'body' apparently synonymous. 'Do they know *who* they are looking for?'

Bassett hesitated only briefly. 'A Mr Philip Read, I understand.'

A second to sink in? Or faint surprise? No *great* relief in her voice. '*Philip. Philip* Read.'

'Do you know of anything which may be of assistance, Mrs Gray?'

'No. No, I don't,' she replied briskly. But when next she spoke she had softened her tone. 'It's just that I have a sister who does foolish things sometimes. She's very good, very sweet, but has the infuriating habit of helping people

who don't wish to be helped, and—oh, I don't know . . .
Philip . . .'

'If you'd care to give me her telephone number—'

'No, no. I mean no, she's not available. She's travelling
to Scotland, I've no idea where she will be at this very
moment. I'll get in touch with her later. Thank you. Thank
you so much. You're very kind . . . I warned her. Over and
over again I warned her . . .'

But this last was almost inaudible, the woman was mum-
bling to herself as she fumbled the receiver back on to its
rest.

Bassett wondered. Was Annette Gray the woman who
had left Bletch Heath village shop in a hurry?

At 8.30 a.m. Bassett rang up Glevebourne Police Station
again.

'Must be telepathy,' Bob Greenaway growled. 'I was
about to phone you. What's this about you snooping into
the Bletch Heath case?'

'Is it a case, Bob?'

'Dunno, frankly. People go missing every day of the week,
often voluntarily. What's your interest?'

Bassett improvised. 'Last night—a neighbour who
thought the car fitted the description of a lady-friend's.
Today—me, plain old curiosity.' Neither was altogether a
lie.

Bassett waited. It came: Bob's snort. Followed by an
exaggerated sigh of resignation. 'Might as well give you
what we've got, I suppose; save you having to wheedle
it out of me. Ready? We were notified at lunch-time
yesterday. Car on a lay-by, et cetera, thought to have
been there since last Saturday. Evidence seems to support
this. Registered owner: Mr Philip Read, home address in
Cheltenham.

'Car not listed as stolen. Locked when found. Tidily
parked, no skid marks. Petrol in tank. Started on the button.

Nothing about it therefore to suggest it had been abandoned—meaning ditched—by owner or thief.

'Folded fawn-coloured gent's raincoat on the back seat.
Flask of coffee, three-quarters full, and plastic sandwich box
containing cheese and digestive biscuits on the front seat;
front passenger seat. In the glovebox: pocket torch, fruit
gums, and a variety of advertising pamphlets. In the
raincoat pockets: gent's handkerchief, library ticket, and a
receipt for a doll.'

'A *doll*?'

'Yep. Receipt's with the lab,' Bob Greenaway said. 'Off
a till roll nearly dry of ink. We have a date: last Saturday's.
A price: £24.95. And the word "Doll". Lab's trying to get
us more, name of the shop, for instance. Read might have
chatted to the shop assistant, indicated who the doll was
for. He's no children of his own.'

'The doll wasn't in the Datsun, I take it.'

Affirmed. 'Cheltenham began investigations their end last
night,' Bob said. 'The man hasn't been reported missing, but
his wife is out of town. He's a social worker. On long weekend
leave, due back this morning. Office doesn't know why he was
in Bletch Heath. As far as they are aware, he had no case in
Bletch Heath or environs; they're checking.'

'Wife not at home, you say. Any mystery attached?'
Bassett inquired.

'Only in so far as we're still trying to locate her. She's on
a business course somewhere. Planning to open an old
people's home, apparently, has to get her sums right first.
They're a private couple, divulge little about themselves.
Next-door neighbour thinks the wife is in Manchester, but
can't swear to it.

'Which brings us back to the doll,' Bob said. 'Cat's away,
mice will play? Lady-friend with a little girl? Parked in the
lay-by to avoid leaving his car outside the lady's house for
all the world to comment upon? His colleagues maintain
that he and his wife are OK, haven't been married all that

long and are still a bit lovey-dovey; but they've only been in Cheltenham for three years. Moved from Halesowen, near Dudley. Which is near Birmingham.'

'Meaning not much is known about them.'

'You've got it. Life was less complicated when folk stayed in the same town all their lives.'

Bassett grunted. 'We should talk.'

And then he asked it. 'D'you know his wife's name?' He sought only confirmation: he knew what the answer would be. Confirmation received: the name of Philip Read's wife was Eileen.

'Eileen. Away on a course. Since when, Bob?'

'Since Friday night.' Bob's words were followed by a heavy silence which he somehow initiated; and then broke, saying thoughtfully, 'You thinking what I'm thinking? Wife goes off on her own, husband takes a holiday at the same time—but separately. Is there something there or isn't there?'

Bassett said nothing.

'On the other hand,' Bob said morosely, 'the doll could have been bought for—what do you call people taken under the wing of a social worker? Clients?—could have been bought for a client's child. Deprived. Orphaned. Fostered. Offspring of a single parent . . .'

'Costly casual toy, Bob.'

No virtue in speculating, anyhow. Gather facts.

'I'm off to Cheltenham any minute, Harry. Nice day for it. Andy's staying here. Try not to drag him into mischief while I'm gone!' Mock pain in Bob's voice.

'As if I would,' Bassett reproached cheerfully. 'Who reported the Datsun to you, by the way?'

'Farmworker, Boon's Farm, Bletch Heath. A Kenneth Collier. Saw the car over the weekend and again Monday. Paid no real attention till yesterday, Tuesday, when it dawned on him that the Datsun had been in the same spot for three days. Nothing wrong with that, folks bring their dogs into the country daily for romps, but the car seemed to be accumulating dust, he thought. In fact it was. More than a single day's cobwebs on it. Also, it rained on Sunday evening but the ground underneath the Datsun was dry . . . So, if you'd like to keep beadies peeled. Doll—little girl—possible one-parent family.'

'Big girls like dolls, too,' Bassett observed.

Call ended, Bassett looked up Mrs Gray's address in the telephone directory, and some few minutes later was donning his best country tweeds.

CHAPTER 4

Annette Gray's house was a pretty black-and-white half-timbered cottage of the kind for which Herefordshire is famous. Its garden was large, sprawling, sun-dappled. Green lawns, trees everywhere, oceans of spring flowers in full bloom. Even in the middle of winter the garden must have been eye-catching; today, in the middle of April, it was a picture.

Bassett slowed sufficiently to read the name on the gate: The Blossoms; then drove on to the village shop.

The purchase of tobacco for himself and chocolate for pup entitled him to the information that Mrs Gray and her sister, Olivia Mulholland, were both widows and had bought The Blossoms two years previously; that Mrs Gray had been a children's nanny for most of her working life; and that Mrs Mulholland was a born bossy-boots. Not so much an interferer as an organizer.

She had wanted to organize the Meddlars.

Beefy, with an accusing nose, was the shop-lady's description of Mrs Mulholland; plump, pretty, gentle, described Annette Gray. Lace with, at party-time, a hint of naughty satin.

In his head Bassett aligned The Blossoms with a cheeky picture of two widowed—available—ladies; but this was no time for amusing thoughts, even private ones. The gentle widow, Mrs Gray, was replenishing the water bowl on a birdtable next to a tree of flowering almond when Bassett's Citroën drew up. Lace this morning: at the neck and at the cuff peeping from below the sleeve of a bulky white cardigan; and although her smile was bright he saw anxiety there too.

'Name's Bassett.' He introduced himself cheerfully as he trod the gravel path towards her.

'I thought you might be,' she said graciously. 'Thank you for being so kind on the telephone.' Anxious eyes met his. 'Have they found Philip Read?'

'No . . .'

'And so you want to know what that telephone call of mine was all about.' She smiled with rather more humour now. 'Your cleaning lady's son was right. He said you'd be after me for the rest of the tale.'

'Half a tale does tantalize, Mrs Gray.' Bassett's smile was disarming.

Annette Gray studied him quietly, seemed to like what she saw. 'You're wondering why I thought that car was Eileen's.'

'And why you ran from the shop yesterday quite alarmed, yet—I'm guessing—worried in silence until dawn this morning, when you rang me up. Me, not the police. There has to be a reason.'

'There is, but I'm not sure it would stand up to interrogation.' She looked away, attention diverted by a blackbird's effort to tug a reluctant worm out of the lawn; and back again. 'I put the kettle on before I came out. Will you join me for a cup of tea? Would you mind if we have it in the kitchen? It's still so chilly in the mornings, much warmer in here,' taking him through to French tiles, sculptured units, and the lingering aroma of breakfast—or birdtable—toast.

She busied herself with the tea. 'A yellow Datsun was the car Eileen Read was using last week when she came to see my sister Olivia. I realize now that her own was probably in for servicing or something, and she had borrowed Philip's . . . Why did I run from the shop? I honestly don't know, in retrospect. I certainly wish I hadn't; I'm supposed to be the sensible feet-on-the-ground one.'

Tea brewed, they sat down at a polished table to drink it.

'Why did I wait until this morning to telephone you about

the car?' Annette continued as she tipped milk into china mugs. 'Because even as I was racing home I remembered that Eileen had told Olivia she was going away on a course, and that Philip was on holiday too and might go with her. Therefore the Datsun couldn't possibly be theirs, therefore I could relax. Which I did. Until I woke up in the early hours and couldn't get back to sleep for evil little voices whispering inside my head. In the end I phoned John, your cleaning lady's son, who gets up at four-thirty every morning—and the rest you know.'

'You wouldn't have the venue of the course, would you, Mrs Gray? The police are having difficulty in locating Mrs Read.'

She shook her head. 'I looked. I felt sure Olivia had it somewhere, but I haven't been able to find it.'

Bassett smiled. 'Not to worry. They're bound to find someone who knows where she is. Tell me, you said something on the telephone about your sister helping people. And Philip Read is a social worker . . .'

'I was still thinking of Eileen,' Annette Gray said. 'She's a social worker as well. In fact more so than Philip. I believe he's purely administrative now, if I might make the distinction. I'm sure it was never ever suggested that Philip go to see the Meddlars.' She paused from pouring tea, flicked Bassett a glance. 'I imagine it's fairly common knowledge that my sister Olivia wanted to help a man named Robby Meddlar. You know who I mean?'

'He's a recluse. Lives with his mother.'

'Oh, good.' And a little laugh. 'I have a habit of rabbiting on, taking it for granted that people know what I'm talking about and often they haven't a clue.'

Little laugh returned. 'My wife Mary had the same habit. I used to be quite an expert mind reader.'

'Used to be?'

'Mary died not long after we moved to Oakleigh.'

'I'm sorry.'

'So am I, Mrs Gray.' A moment. Then: 'I think I understand. The mother—Alice Meddlar—has a certain reputation with a shotgun. When you heard about the Datsun
you thought that Eileen had called on the Meddlars and
that something had happened to her. May I ask why you
jumped to that conclusion?'

'Oh . . .' Annette Gray mocked herself. 'Subliminal messages, Mr Bassett. When you are told something often
enough . . .'

'Some of it is guaranteed to sink in. True.' Bassett said it
throwaway. He declined the offer of ginger biscuits, sipped
his tea and let her know it was delicious. Began: 'I'm
intrigued. Reclused mother and son. What prompted your
sister . . . ?' And presently was being told the whole story.

'We hadn't heard of the Meddlars,' Annette explained,
'until last Christmas, when Olivia became involved with
the village party. She saw this strange little lady getting on
our Tuesday shoppers' bus and was naturally curious. Who
was she? Alice Meddlar, she was told. Nobody of that name
on her list. Moreover nobody seemed keen to add the name
to the list. Mystery here, Annette! she said; and little by
little—she can be extremely persuasive—she found out
about Robby.

'She was furious with his mother and her over-possessive
old-fashioned ideas about mental defectives. Too late to do
anything about her, Alice Meddlar, but Robby should be
out in the world, enjoying life, and she, Olivia, was going
to see to it that he did.

'The day before Christmas Eve, however, and before
she'd had time to do anything constructive, Olivia spotted
Mrs Meddlar in Glevebourne with a girl and a baby, which
slowed her down a little. If Robby and his mother had
guests for Christmas they must not live as lonely a life as
we had been led to understand. She had followed them
home, you see.' A wry smile apologized for Olivia's outrage-
ous behaviour. 'Watched them unloading what in her

opinion was definitely shopping for more than two. And where there was a young mother and infant there was bound to be a husband and possibly other members of a family.

'She let it lie for a while. Say a week,' Annette added with dry humour. 'But needless to say, when the girl moved into Forge Cottage in the New Year—her name is Kathy McDonald—Olivia was first to arrive on her doorstep. She had it in mind that she and the girl together might be able to get Robby to a Day Centre or somesuch; an Adult Training Centre, even. I think she spoke to the girl about it two or three times, tentatively.'

'Tentatively,' Bassett said, when Annette stopped to drink tea. 'It wasn't taken up?'

A headshake. 'No. Olivia discovered that the girl was on her own with the baby. And she wasn't at all cooperative. Truthfully, I was glad. We might not think the man's life has quality, I told Olivia, but who are we to judge? After all, he's not exactly a prisoner; and his mother might have her own reasons—very good ones—for keeping him tied to her apron. I thought—hoped—that Olivia would forget the whole idea. But no.' Annette sighed.

'Goodness knows what started it, but Olivia became increasingly more concerned about Kathy McDonald and the baby than about Robby. For one thing, she found out that Kathy wasn't a great-niece of Alice's, which was the rumour when the girl first arrived. In fact Kathy is no relation of Alice's whatsoever. She was coming to move into Forge Cottage in time for Christmas, got herself lost, and Alice took her in.

'She's a stranger! An innocent! Olivia said. And there's that dear little baby to consider! It came out that Olivia had seen a man she took to be Robby Meddlar peering in at one of Kathy's windows when the girl was out. Olivia went to speak to him and he fled. Also she had picked up a whisper about Robby's background. His father. And Robby having possibly inherited bad blood. Something about his father having been a psychopath, a convicted killer—'

'A *killer*?'

'Oh, I didn't take it seriously,' Annette Gray said matter-of-factly. 'At least, I thought I hadn't.' Referring obliquely to her flight from the shop. 'John didn't either when I mentioned it to him. The Meddlars have lived on the edge of the village for a quarter of a century, almost as long as John, and he'd not heard of it. She'd had her leg pulled, he said. Some wag, fed up with her poking her nose in.'

Bassett nodded to himself: he could imagine.

'Nevertheless her concern was genuine,' Annette said loyally. 'Concern for Kathy and her baby, and what she thought could be an unhealthy friendship with Robby.'

'And that was why she eventually contacted the Social Services.'

'No, no, not the Services. Officially she might have done more harm than good. She had a word with Mrs Read, Eileen. They had worked together years ago, before Eileen was married. Until we came to live here Olivia had been heavily involved with voluntary work of one kind or another: hospitals, Samaritans, Citizens Advice.' She shrugged lightly. 'Which was why I was never very sympathetic to this Cause of hers. She's not occupied enough here. I suspected her of *looking* for something to worry about.

'Anyhow, she asked Eileen to call on the girl. A casual visit, no pressure. Make it a sort of welfare visit, to check up on the baby, and if Kathy was amenable sound her out about Robby. Eileen was well trained to handle it, apparently.'

'Do you know the outcome of the visit, Mrs Gray?'

'I don't know that Eileen had got round to it.'

'But you thought she had. You thought she might have visited Kathy McDonald and gone on to the Meddlars.'

'Mm.' Meaning yes. 'Until I remembered Eileen's course. And something else . . .' Annette faltered.

'Yes?' Bassett prompted.

'I was going to say that I *had* half-hoped she was going to let the matter drop. Something she said last week after Eileen had been to see her. She was looking through some snapshots Eileen had left for her, deep in thought. Suddenly she gazed up into space, and—I think I may have made a terrible mistake, Annette, she said.'

'She didn't explain?'

'No. She put the snaps away and went to bed. I confess I don't always listen to Olivia as attentively as I might. But I did hear her say that. I took it to mean that Eileen had talked some sense into her. As I had tried to do and failed. I—' She broke off with a small cry. 'The snapshots! They're in the drawer of the telephone table. We keep most of our snaps there.'

Bassett quickly finished his tea and followed her into the hall.

'Yes, here it is.' She pointed to the number written on the green snapshot envelope. 'I think you'll find that's the telephone number of Eileen's hotel.'

'May I phone it through to the police?'

'Please do.'

That done, Bassett thanked the lady for her help, and for the tea, and prepared to leave. 'Have you heard from your sister yet? Travelling to Scotland, you said.'

'To Fort William. She left on Monday. A relation of her second husband's. She spends a week or so with him every year, but she never rushes the journey. Puts up at an hotel or two en route, choosing them as fancy takes her.'

She smiled an apologetic smile. 'I've no desire to try and contact her unless forced. She would leave her car and be on the first train back. I love Olivia dearly, Mr Bassett, but I also thoroughly enjoy the rare occasions I have the house to myself. I will ring her up, I promise, if and when necessary. At the moment, what do I say to her? I've never met Philip Read. I don't actually *know* either Philip or Eileen. Eileen is Olivia's friend, not mine. They could have lent the car to someone. It could have been stolen from outside their house by a thief who knew they weren't at home . . . Or, if Philip *didn't* go with Eileen, he could have his own private reasons for being in this part of the world, couldn't he?'

Bassett agreed. 'He could indeed.'

He said nothing about the doll.

CHAPTER 5

Forge Cottage was reminiscent of Bassett's own: semi-wild garden, old orchard, ancient hedges thick with blossom, dainty wild daffodils and here and there early bluebells; rabbits and birds an accepted feature of the scenery.

At first glance he thought he might be about to meet Robby Meddlar: man's cap, check shirt and denim work jeans. When he drew closer he saw not a man but the unmistakable shape of a woman. She was lugging a bulging sack up a grassy path. 'Won't be a sec!' she called.

The impulse was to go and relieve her of the load, but hardly was Bassett inside the gate than she had relinquished the sack; plus raggedy gauntlets and what looked to be a small handsaw. He watched her lean over the pram by the porch and delight its occupant with laughing baby-talk; then she was tripping towards him, cheeks flushed and sweaty, eyes bright though questioning. Early twenties, Bassett calculated, politely raising his hat.

Happy-natured, too: she saw the funny side when he said mock-awkwardly, 'I was only passing. Blame pup, she's inquisitive,' pup promptly giving credence to the fib by tugging on her lead and stretching her neck two miles long towards the pram. 'Sunny Jim, there,' Bassett said.

'Oh yes, Michael.' Not a girl-baby, good. 'She's so big!' the girl exclaimed, stooping down to fondle the labrador 'Are you sure she's still a pup?'

Bassett chuckled. 'She thinks she is.'

The girl laughed. 'That's what matters! Aren't you lovely? You're a sweetie.' Cuddle begot cuddle, naturally.

She had been wood-gathering, Kathy McDonald informed Bassett conversationally. 'There's a mountain of wood in the old orchard, and I've discovered that even rotten wood that's been lying on the ground for ages burns well as long as the fire has a good base. Also, it's easier to saw,' she said impishly.

Bassett regarded her quietly and marvelled: she was positively thriving on hard work.

He leaned back on his heels, rubbed his nose with a knuckle—a self-conscious gesture that occasionally was feigned—studied her while she gazed back at him quizzically, and suddenly jabbed at the air between them. 'I've seen you before! In Glevebourne. Shopping. You were carrying the baby in a harness on your chest!' It was true, he did recollect seeing her; the harness had caught his attention, he had thought: How sensible. 'You had an elderly lady with you.' *She* he hadn't seen, but no matter, the girl was nodding, all eyes.

'Mrs Meddlar,' she said.

'Mrs Meddlar. From whom you are learning country lore. Or were you born a countrywoman?'

'Townie, I'm afraid. My paternal grandparents used to live in a village when I was little, but they had pavements and street lighting; it was nothing like this, this is real country.'

And she loved it. 'Do you live hereabouts?'

'Matter of fact, I've retired to a cottage not unlike yours in Oakleigh, six miles thataway.'

'Oh.'

'I have an orchard same as yours—doesn't every country dwelling in Herefordshire boast an apple orchard! I had pigs clear mine of undergrowth. Far less damaging to the earth than bulldozers, less work for me than scythe and mower, and—' lowering his voice—'pigs fertilize as they go,' he said delicately.

'Do you still have them?' she asked, amused.

'My last two were Gloucester Old Spots. Passed them on to a farmer who keeps rare breeds. I fancy they are better off with him than with me.'

'Oh, I'm sure that's debatable. I've no ambitious plans for my orchard though, I'm only tidying it.' Hence the 'logging'. She had picked that word up from her friend Robby, she said. He had taught her how to use an axe and saw properly. 'You'd laugh if you could see my miniature axe and saw next to Robby's huge ones. But then I only cut tiny logs. Twigs really!'

Bassett laughed anyway. He thought her charming.

The postman arrived. They chatted. 'Well, best push on. Nothing new on that car they found abandoned, is there?' the postman said cheerfully as he was leaving.

As cheerfully Bassett replied, 'Haven't heard anything.'

'I did hear something . . .' Bassett appeared to confide in the girl as they waved the red van off. 'Friend of mine thinks it belongs to health visitors. Trouble is no one seems to know who they were visiting. Would they have been here?'

The girl's head moved slowly from side to side.

'I thought all new mothers had visits,' Bassett said. 'No?'

'Not necessarily, no.'

'I wonder,' Bassett said thoughtfully. 'Wasn't there some talk about Mrs Mulholland and Mr Meddlar?'

'Robby? Getting Robby to a Centre, you mean.' A nod. 'Mrs Mulholland did approach me some time ago. She annoyed me though, frankly, she was so bombastic I didn't encourage her. She would go on about *defectives*; as if they were a race apart. I told her Robby isn't a mental defective, he's a person who's different . . . Is that why Mrs Gray came?' Kathy asked rhetorically. 'Mrs Gray came to see me.'

'When was this?'

'When she came? This morning, early.'

'What did she say?' Bassett inquired.

'Similar to you. Something about a welfare officer coming here and going on to the Meddlars. A Mr Read. She said nothing about a car. And she said Saturday. Which seems an odd day for a welfare officer to call. I would expect routine calls to be made on weekdays. Is something wrong? I hope people haven't been listening to Mrs Mulholland.'

'Listening?' Bassett said, as they eyed each other.

'I think the woman is neurotic, honestly I do. Robby is as gentle as a lamb. Sweet, kind. You would think, for example, that someone who spends as much time outdoors as he does would be blasé about the harsher aspects of nature, wouldn't you? Robby isn't. He feels it very deeply when he finds a dead bird or badger or fox or anything; can't rest until he's dug a grave and buried them.' Kathy looked away and back again. 'What is this about a car?'

Bassett made light of it. 'A car found in a lay-by. Could be stolen. Teenagers joy-riding, perhaps.' He looked down at pup who had flopped down on the grass and was staring at him mournfully. 'We'd better finish our romp or I'll never hear the last of it! Mustn't hold you up any longer either, Mrs—?'

'McDonald. Kathy McDonald.'

'Henry Bassett.' Touching his hat. 'I hate the name Henry; don't mind you addressing me as Harry; but I answer best to plain Bassett. May we come again, please, Kathy McDonald?'

'You must!' Her eyes were shining once more.

CHAPTER 6

Where to next? To Tree Tops, current home of Alice and
Robby Meddlar? Or to Bletch House, where Alice had once
worked as lady's maid? In the event, the first person he
spoke to advised Bassett that the once lively Bletch House
had been relegated to rich city gent's toy, but if he would
like to see the caretaker-cum-gardener, a chap named Clem,
best he went around noon to the lodge; Clem would be there
partaking of his lunch.

So the Meddlar homestead won the toss, so to speak.

He left Bletch Heath by one route and re-entered the
village environs from a different direction, following the
route mapped out for him by Andy Miller: main country
road for two miles after the war memorial, turn left after
the brook into Cooper's Lane—unmarked, so watch out
for it—then on for half a mile to the lay-by. Several
vehicles including a police personnel carrier littered verges
sporadically beyond the turn-off, but no one impeded
Bassett's passage.

The lay-by was small, a one-car parking slot, a bite
taken out of rocky hillside, with brambles, wild flowers and
woodland rising on all three sides. It remained cordoned
off, although the Datsun had long since been towed away.
Bassett got out of his car to examine tyre marks; then drove
on until the lane began to curve and widen. Here he slowed,
looking back . . . on a little further, to look back once more
. . . and brake.

There it was behind him: the track to Tree Tops.

He drove on, turned the car round in the opening to a
field of rape, left the car there, and with pup on a lead
started walking. On his right, a wooded rise on the other
side of which, perhaps a mile as the crow flew, was Kathy

McDonald's cottage; on his left, flat arable land, silver roofs of farm buildings glinting above a low mist in the middle distance.

He reached the foot of the track. Alice Meddlar, recluse, had chosen shrewdly: running obliquely from the lane, and partly concealed by overgrown greenery, the entrance to the track appeared derelict; a drunken letter-box, weather-worn Keep Out sign, and poker-worked nameboard, Tree Tops, mere relics. You might pass a score of times and not notice them. Why should you when there was no related dwelling in sight?

Slowly up the track, pup strangely no more anxious than he to go crashing into undergrowth and last year's dry bracken. Crackles of movement all around, but only when a pheasant rose into the air with a fearful clatter was Bassett able to pinpoint the position of uniformed searchers. Not here, in the woods higher up.

They were searching for a body. For the moment he was interested in tyre marks.

To no avail, alas: the wheel ruts he followed were gravel-bottomed and so retained no tyre prints of value.

The track was long, an uphill trudge. Several times Bassett experienced the uncomfortable sensation that he was being watched. Every now and then he would halt abruptly, swivel; see no one. Pup too stood still once or twice and seemed to listen, sniff for a scent, dart glances at some phantom. Rabbits, Bassett assured himself when pup lowered her head to peer into a tunnel worked at ground level through a thicket. Yet when he glimpsed a chimney rising from trees up ahead he was tempted to say: That's it, we've found the place, we'll know where to come next time! and retrace his steps.

He plodded on. Trees fell back, the ground opened out to resemble a small farmyard. The large brick house had once upon a time stood four-square; but barns and outbuildings had been tacked on haphazardly so that now it must

be described as rambling. Tired, dusty, but no hovel. Neat
paths ran from door to chicken barn to water butts, and to
a partly enclosed paved area where clothing hung from a
line. Flowers flourished randomly in tubs and pots; the
picture was pleasant.

'Hello! Anybody there?' Bassett called.

A sociable rooster replied with a cheerful crow. A tabby
cat roused from a nap in a sunny corner by the butts yawned,
stretched; and would have come purring to rub itself against
his feet, he felt sure, if he hadn't had pup with him. And a
woman came into view from the direction of one of the
barns.

Good grief! Truly Bassett hadn't known what to expect.
Certainly not this, an apparition dolled up to the nines all
colours of the rainbow. She was sweeping up with a yard
broom, swishing it back and forth with vigour, her spindly
legs flying; and she was singing the hymn 'Onward, Christian Soldiers' for her own entertainment at the top of her
voice. She obviously hadn't heard his hello, nor did she see
him now; she carried on about her business.

Later Bassett would say that he imagined she owned
trunks full of long-ago fashionable clothes, and that she
played lucky dip with them every morning. Today she had
pulled out a magenta crêpe sensation, a black astrakhan
bolero, brown suede boots, white net gloves with blue bows
on them; and on her head she wore a World War Two
airman's flying helmet. Her hair was hennaed, and she wore
the helmet with the ear flaps unbuttoned so that tufts of
frizzy hair stuck out of the earphone holes. Another tuft
embraced her forehead. Her cheeks were rouged, a rosebud
mouth had been painted on, ignoring the corners. She
looked a mess, but oh, the body language!

What should he do, disappear? Or wait? Make a noise?
Move? She spotted him. The broom went up in the air
defensively. At least it was a broom, not a shotgun.

Bassett was quick to smile. 'Sorry if I startled you,' he

said genially. 'I was passing, wondered if you had Free-Range eggs for sale.'

'Eggs? Eggs are for eating, not selling.' She stared. Bright little birdlike eyes. 'Didn't ask you to come,' she rasped. 'Didn't ask him to come here, did I?'— to some invisible being sitting on her left shoulder.

'No eggs. Oh, well.' Bassett thanked her, took his leave. 'Brave thing we did there, Babydog,' he muttered to pup. Although Alice Meddlar hadn't seemed a bad old thing; he'd seen worse.

He glanced back twice: once, to see her gazing after him; once, to glimpse a tall shadowy figure at her side, a large felling axe in his hands.

Mindful of Bob Greenaway's idea about Philip Read and a lady-friend, Bassett trained his thoughts for a spell on the farm beyond the rape fields. Suppose the man had parked his car on the lay-by and walked to his lady across the fields. Suppose he had been taken ill and stopped over . . . No. Unlikely. The lady, if not Read himself, would have been wise to the interest shown in the Datsun by now, and would have claimed it.

All the same, as there was an hour still to go to noon Bassett headed for the farm, setting a course round the perimeter of the fields. The walk took twenty minutes.

The farm was Boon's. Bassett checked up his notebook for the name of the man who had notified the police about the Datsun, then went looking for him. Cattle shed: farmyard smells, nothing more. Chicken barn . . . He and pup were sticky-beaking from the barn entrance when a voice behind them cried affably, 'Nobody in!'

Bassett turned to smile at the workman ambling up to him, a man with pale blond hair, weathered cheeks, and an odd—blind?—right eye. 'Mr Collier?'

The man replied no. 'Ken's popped home.'

'When will he be back?'

'Well now . . .' The 'popped home' and 'nobody in' were
figures of speech. Ken Collier had gone home to change
and the owner of the farm, Mr Boon, was in but not available; there was a funeral from the farm today: the farmer's
wife.

'Went of a sudden, like. Stroke on Friday, never woke
up. Took Saturday.'

Bassett uttered condolences and moved to withdraw; but
the man stayed with him and was disposed to chat. Thus
Bassett learnt that the deceased Mrs Boon had been eighty-
six years old; that there were no daughters or daughters-in-
law living at the farm, nor dairymaids or kitchen staff; and
that Mrs Collier, Ken's wife, had nursed the old lady from
first to last, had been with her when she died, and had spent
the remainder of the weekend consoling Mr Boon, meeting
visitors come to pay their respects, and generally acting as
housekeeper.

'Just you and Mr Collier work here?' Bassett said. 'Small
farm then . . .'

'We engage some casual help but mostly it's me and Ken
do the work, aye—and the old man does the moaning.'
This, with half a grin. 'Keeps us kicking over. Not a bad
life all in all.' Clearly content with his lot.

'You live where?' Bassett inquired, friendly-fashion.

'Here. Took me in when I was a lad, and I've been here
ever since. Never wanted to be anywhere else.'

'Married?' Bassett smiled.

'Never got round to it,' the man said shyly. 'You know
where Ken lives, do you?' They had reached the space
between farm and rape field. 'Over there. Set back from the
road.' He reared his head. 'Can't see much from here.'

'I'll find it. Won't trouble him today, though.'

'Aye. Sad day.' The man sighed. 'Sad day for all of us.'
His mouth drooped for a second; then he jerked his chin,
squinted to gaze into the distance. 'Cars! Won't take me
but five minutes to get ready—'

'Thank you for your help,' Bassett called as the man sped off.

'You're welcome,' the man called back.

Dead end? Bassett wondered. Appeared to be. If Mrs Collier was the only woman here, and she had been tending a sick old lady and then her husband . . . The only thing that was odd under the circumstances was Mr Collier's noticing the Datsun so often over the weekend; but on reflection this was probably no more unusual than this other chap's last-minute dash to don his funeral suit: work on a farm had to go on.

Noon. As Bassett got out of his Citroën on one side of the lodge gates at Bletch House a fresh-faced elderly gent wearing boiler suit, red neckerchief and cotton cap rode a lawnmower to a halt on the other.

The lodge gates were open. 'Are you Clem?' Bassett inquired amiably as the man dismounted.

'That's me. Clement by name, clement by nature!'

Bassett motioned. 'Garden does you credit. Do it all yourself, I've been told.'

'That I do.' Modesty aside. 'Hard work, but if you keeps at it . . . Mainly trees and lawns now, though.'

Bassett inclined his head. 'I know you, don't I?' No pretence, the face was vaguely familiar.

'I know you, any road.' The gardener chortled. 'Friend o' Tod Arkwright's. We met at the County Show coupla years back. Don't reckon as how we was properly introduced, mind—'

'Bassett.' He stuck out a hand.

'Bassett! Ar, that's the name. Wouldn't've expected you to recognize me, I looks different when I'm dressed up. Have to go out now and again, I says, otherwise nobody'd know I had any decent clothes!'

They laughed; chinwagged; in the main about Bletch House in the days of Mrs Popple, the former owner.

'Any of the old indoor staff around, Clem?'

The gardener looked at Bassett knowingly. 'Anybody who was here with Alice Meddlar, you mean. You're a-seeing into that car business. Tod said as how you might come a-calling. Reckoned you'd be on to it if'n there were a mystery. Have they found the driver?'

'They hadn't half an hour ago.'

The gardener nodded abstractedly. 'Old harpy, they reckon, our Alice.'

He looked down at his feet and up again. 'Had the young fella here as reported the motor, fetched a load o' flowers for the church. Ar, for the funeral.'

'Mrs Boon's.'

'Ar. Snapped like a carrot—here one day, gone the next. I'd've been a-going 'cepting they're keeping it private. Funerals is thought nowt of to what they used to be . . . Face on him to curdle the milk, the young fella. Went into the police station just to mention it, he says; never meant for them to turn up at his house asking daft questions and upsetting his missus.'

'Routine questions, Clem, I dare say.'

'That's what I told him. Stands to reason, I said; they'll be a-knocking on everybody's door, I shouldn't wonder . . . He reckons they ought to look in that woodshed at Alice's place.'

A silence fell.

The young fella reckoned? Or Clem reckoned?

'What do you think, Clem?' Bassett asked quietly.

'I think you find the one as is missing, then you come again to see me. You, mind, nobody else.'

Philip Read's body was found later that afternoon. Not in a woodshed but in a grave in the woods.

CHAPTER 7

Bassett stared down at the body of Philip Read. His wounds had not been made by a shotgun. 'Looks as if someone bashed him across the face with a four-by-two,' Andy Miller had informed him on the telephone. Now the young sergeant said with feeling, 'Poor bloke.'

Bassett stared for a long time. If this had been a church-yard instead of woodland he might have been murmuring, 'Somebody forgot the coffin.' For the dead man, fully clothed in grey suit and collar and tie, was lying on his back, legs straight, arms folded across his chest, for all the world as though he had been laid out by an undertaker. Nor was the grave a hastily dug hollow scraped out by a murderer in a hurry: whoever had buried the body had ex-cavated a neat professional-looking grave, rectangular and deep.

'Who found him, Andy?'

'One of the search team. WPC Rogers.' The young sergeant produced a polaroid photograph. 'That's the grave when it was found. Look, guvnor—'

Bassett looked. The photograph showed a roughly coffin-shaped mound, neatened and strewn with tree cut-tings and twigs; and *something else*. 'See?' Andy said.

A bunch of daffodils and wood anemones had been placed on the grave. Some had since been scattered by wildlife, but the distinct basis of a bunch remained.

'I've a feeling that if we looked hard enough we'd find a cross fashioned from twigs,' Andy said with a grim smile.

Bassett muttered, 'Rowan and birch to ward off the evil eye.'

The second photograph showed the grave after the cover-ing soil had been scraped off: the body was neatly wrapped in a blanket. A very old blanket, intrinsically clean, Bassett noted.

A third photograph was of the body when both edges of the blanket had been opened out: in other words, the body as it was now.

Bassett studied all three photographs once more, handed them back. 'The Reads are a two-car family, Andy. They may have gone on this course of Mrs Read's together. Could have lent the car to a friend   '

'Don't think so, guvnor. Cheque-book and credit cards in the dead man's pockets belong to C. Philip Read. Incidentally, he wasn't robbed, not of money anyway. Five tenners in his pocket. I mean his wallet.'

'And I doubt very much if he was killed here in the woods, Andy.'

'The blanket?'

'Mm. Suggests he was killed elsewhere and carried here.' Inevitably Bassett recalled Kathy McDonald's saying of Robby, *He feels it deeply when he finds a dead bird or badger . . . or anything; can't rest until he's dug a grave and buried them.* But he said nothing.

Footprints? Drag marks? Nothing useful, Andy told him. Bassett surveyed the scene himself: springy grass in the grave area, leafmould elsewhere; even heavy-footed coppers had made little impression. As for trails through spring's wild flowers and summer's new shoots, they could have been made by woodland creatures, foxes and badgers. At this stage, that is; a minute search would continue later.

'What we're after now,' Andy said, cocking a look towards where the photographer and team were working, 'is the dead man's briefcase. Apparently a neighbour of Read's saw him leaving his house on Saturday morning, swears he had his briefcase with him. We can't put great store on that; if he leaves every day carrying the briefcase the neighbour will have seen it whether Read had it or not, if you follow me.' He shrugged.

'But if he did have it with him we can assume he wasn't just gallivanting,' Bassett said.

'Depends, guvnor. If he was in Bletch Heath for a bit on the side a briefcase would have its uses. He could be the insurance man as far as *her* neighbours would be concerned.'

Bassett nodded assent. 'Point taken. Any advance on the wife?'

Located, Andy said. 'Doesn't know we've found a body and that her first task will be to identify him formally, poor woman. Bob spoke to her on the blower, explained about the car and so on. She didn't wait to hear any more, said she was on her way and put the phone down. So we couldn't ask her about this—'

Andy had taken out his notebook. Philip Read's desk had thrown up a scribbled note:

'Tree Tops—Meddlar. McDonald—Forge.'

'They've no idea what it means, guvnor, but one of Read's colleagues recollects a phone call Read received on Friday afternoon from his wife. From what he overheard, the colleague gathered that Read was being reminded about an errand or chore he had to do. Quote: I won't forget it, leave it with me . . . McDonald is a name I've got to look into. Several in the phone book but none round here. Unless you . . . ?' An eyebrow arched.

Bassett felt in his pocket for his pipe. 'I'd say it's all academic at the moment, Andy. Let's wait and hear what the dead man's wife has to tell us. Doc been?'

Dr Jim McPherson, police surgeon and friend of Bassett's.

Been and gone, said Andy. 'Said I was to give you his best. Didn't want to hang around, he's got a bad dose of 'flu. But he had to come himself, wouldn't send his locum: you know Doc, likes to see a body *in situ*! Couldn't tell us much, but confirmed that Read could have been dead for three or four days. Which ties in with Saturday and the length of time the Datsun was left standing. No car keys on Read, by the way.'

Bassett made a mental note.

'And Bob's on the way back from Cheltenham,' Andy said. 'Should be here any minute.'

Bassett was silent while he filled his pipe. He pocketed his tobacco pouch. 'I won't stay, Andy. This Meddlar and McDonald, though. Wouldn't mind being in on it if they come in for a bit of questioning.'

Andy opened his mouth to speak; closed it again; saluted. 'I'll pass the message on, guvnor. I take it you'll be doing a bit of moseying.' Straight-faced.

Bassett deliberately misunderstood. He poked the young sergeant playfully in the chest with the stem of his pipe. 'Wouldn't dream of tramping about in these woods, Andy. Might snag me breeches, then where would I be? Suspect number one!'

Shortly afterwards, pipe still unlit, Bassett was winding his way down the path worn up from the lane by Andy and his team.

A green pick-up truck carrying fence posts and rolls of chain-link fencing trundled by as Bassett hit gravel. The truck ground to a halt, the driver got out. He was tall, in his late thirties or thereabouts, wore the clothes of a working farmer, was coarse-featured but not unhandsome; and shambled up to Bassett glancing to the left and to the right, hands in pockets, shoulders hunched as if he were shy or self-conscious.

Not about his appearance, surely; no man who wore his hair in a plait could be that unsure of himself.

'Sent you packing, have they?'

'Sorry?'

The man tossed a glance. 'Bit of a shemozzle going on up there, isn't there? I wondered if they'd found the driver of the Datsun. Only I'm the one who notified them,' he added informatively, and not without a touch of self-importance.

'Ah!' Bassett's interest sharpened. 'I fancy they might have found *some*thing, Mr—er—'

'Collier. Ken Collier. From the farm over there.' The man smiled, frowned, inspected Bassett up and down, all in the space of a second. 'You police?'

'Was. Retired now.'

'But still keen, eh?' The farmworker's gaze swept the woods. 'I was in two minds whether to report it or not. Thought somebody'd turn up and bless me.'

'Been there a day or two, though, hadn't it?' Bassett made it sound as if that excused him.

'Three days all told. Since Saturday.' He shifted his gaze to Bassett. 'And you hear of such goings-on these days. Every time you switch on the telly. Woman disappeared here, another found murdered there. And there's nearly always a car mixed up in it.'

'Why do you think it's a woman?'

'Well . . .' The man walked a yard, scuffing his feet. Pushed his shoulders up an inch higher while he glanced at Bassett. 'Tell the truth, we did wonder, the wife and me. Do you know Mrs Mulholland?'

'Mrs Gray's sister.'

'That's her. The wife thought she saw the Datsun outside Mrs Mulholland's one day last week. Woman got out of it, she said, carrying a sort of district-nurse bag. Health visitor, the wife thought. Tied it in with Mrs Mulholland going on about that Robby bloke. Robby Meddlar. And lately the girl who's moved into Forge Cottage. You know, one thing and another. We wondered if Robby Meddlar'd been making a nuisance of himself with the girl and Mrs Mulholland had stepped in and got on to the authorities.'

'Has he made a nuisance of himself before?'

'I wouldn't know. We've only lived here eighteen months. But chaps like that . . . We had a neighbour where I used to live when I was a kid. Little Fred. He loved the girls. A kind word from a pretty face and Little Fred was

there, couldn't get rid of him. Not that I said anything of
that to the police, mind. You don't like to, do you?' The
man flicked a brief smile. 'Enough people out to brew
trouble for others without me adding to them.'

He had continued to intersperse what he was saying with
glances up at the woods—nothing to see. Now, however,
there was. 'Aye-aye,' he exclaimed, 'things are stirring.
Here's where I push off.'

And was gone; leaving Bassett also to wonder.

CHAPTER 8

'They've found a body, Clem.' Bassett lowered himself on to the garden bench seat next to the gardener.

'So you've come to me as I told you to.'

'I can wait if you've other things to do.'

'No, nothing better'n this for the minute, seeing as it's knocking-off time any road. I often sit here a-looking. A-looking and a-thinking. What would we do without our gardens?' A calloused hand encompassed what was indeed a lovely panoramic view. 'Who—?'

Bassett drew him a brief picture of the man whose body had been found, omitting details of the grave.

'Clobbered him.' Bassett heard mild surprise, watched Clem remove his cloth hat, an automatic gesture of respect, perhaps, and hold it limply between his knees. 'And we know who they'll be a-wanting for it.'

The cap swung like a weary pendulum twice, then the gardener straightened and placed the cap beside him on the bench. 'Not many'll speak up for Alice, so I'll do a bit of it meself.' Clem's chin jerked. 'What do you know about her?'

'That she worked at Bletch House for Mrs Popple. Married. Left the area. Turned up again with her son twenty-five years ago.'

'That she did. Turned up with a little lad, no husband, no explanation; and it were months afore anybody recognized her or found out where she and the boy was a-living—'

The gardener interrupted himself. 'That were one of young Kathy McDonald's questions; you know Kathy? She asked me why no one had made friends with Alice. Seemed to worry the lass; started a-hearing a few tales, I reckon . . . 'T'weren't so peculiar, I told the lass. Alice had been gone twenty years, ar, left here when she was thirty-odd, been

back twenty-five years, and she's near enough eighty now,
nearer Tod Arkwright's age than mine. Any road, you go
back to anywhere after a length away, I told her, and you'll
find a whole new generation. Been a war to get back on our
feet from, people had come, people had gone, including Mrs
Popple.

'But the bottom and both ends of it, Bassett, was that
Alice had come here as a lass over the heads of girls in the
village. Many a village lass had been a-hoping to get the
job Alice got, and her an outsider, if you get my meaning;
and ill-feeling in them days seldom got mended. Got on
with the men, but oh, not most o' the women. All the same,
if she'd a-knocked on a door and said it's me, I'm back. If
she'd only been civil! She weren't. Trotted round in a pony
and trap, her and the boy, nose in the air, so that everybody
was puzzled as to who the fine lady was.'

Tod Arkwright had been the first to figure her out, the
gardener went on. Tod worked on the Clarkson Hall Estate
in Oakleigh (Bassett's village) in Alice's day, and the
Popples and Clarksons had been friends; Tod, as gamekeeper's assistant, used to be present at Hunt Meetings
and Shoots; he'd seen a fair bit of Alice.

Twenty-five years ago he had seen the fine lady out in
the trap, and— 'Daft lot! It's Alice Spicer, as was!' None of
them remembered her married name, if they had ever known
it. Tod had tried to pay respects; and Frank Stone, who had
been a gardener's boy and sweet on Alice; he'd sneaked her
many a posy. Inoffensive as they come, old Frank—gone
now, o'course; but Alice sent him packing. Not the same
Alice, he informed everybody. Not a kind word in her.

So they'd let her get on with it.

'Rumours drifted all round,' gardener Clem continued.
'Alice were supposed to have married money, some said
she'd ended up penniless again. Others said as how her
husband must've died and her'd come back to flaunt her
wealth—that place of hers being tumbledown but bigger'n

anything any of us had growed up in. You know how it is, tongues a-wagging fifty to the dozen. Lot o' twaddle, most of it, an' all.'

He paused, ruminated, said sentimentally, 'I remember a-seeing the two of 'em, the boy would've been seven or eight. Had him dressed smashing. Proper little Lord Fauntleroy. And Alice, very Lady of the Manor. Long pale blue dress and hat. Ar, with ribbons on it. Credit where due, they looked a bit of all right then.

'Suddenly, though—down comes the shutters. Never seed the pony and trap again, only clapped eyes on our Alice once in a blue moon, and word went round as how her boy were a simon.

'But now, this is what I wanted to tell you. When Alice got wed she shut the door firmly behind her. The only one she kept in touch with were a lass named Edith Turner, wed an American airman, went to America.'

He had never expected to see Edith again, Clem said; but lo and behold, about twelve years ago Edith had come to England for a holiday and had looked in at Bletch House. She was trying to track down Alice, Alice's letters having ceased abruptly—at about the same time, when Clem worked it out, as Alice and her boy had returned to Bletch Heath. Edith had been to Alice's old home, in Warwickshire he thought, hadn't been able to trace Alice's whereabouts, but from a former neighbour had learnt that her husband was said to be a convicted murderer.'

'A murderer?' At last Bassett spoke.

'That were the tale Edith got,' Clem said sadly. 'Killed a man, then went off his trolley. Couldn't tell me no more'n that because the neighbour didn't know any more herself. They'd never mixed—Alice and her man—and they spent more time away from home than in it. The murder had happened one time when they was away, up in Newcastle, she'd heard tell.'

A few moments' contemplation, and Clem went on, 'I

couldn't believe it. I reckoned we'd have heard summat ourselves. But when I got to figuring, we'd never knowed *who* Alice were a-marrying. She'd left, gone off to get wed. To a man of standing, a man of property, was all she'd ever tell anyone. So if the murder had been in the papers or on the TV or wireless we'd have been none the wiser, if you get my meaning.

'Any road, after Edith had gone I went a-calling on Alice. Felt sorry for the woman. I figured as she'd thought we did know about her trouble, hadn't been quick with any kind word, and what she'd been a-doing when she paraded her little lad—she'd been a-telling us: Here's my son! see, he's no monster! Take a good look, then leave us be.

'Took me a bit longer to work out why she'd come here, if it'd been me I'd have cleared off to where nobody knowed me. But I reckon the poor 'ooman had to come here. She wanted no truck with us, but it were a comfort to her to be in familiar surroundings. And, as I said, I went a-calling.

'No sympathy, too late for that. Told her about the trips we got up. Pantomimes at Christmas, trips to the seaside in the summer. You wants to come! I said. I'm on my own, my missus, bless her, passed on a while back. Company for me, Alice, I said. I'll take the lad along of me. Keep an eye on him, I meant.'

Bassett nodded: he understood.

'Alice wouldn't have none of it. They lived their own lives, she said, no bother to anybody, and Robby were happy as long as his routine weren't upset. Best I leave things be. Polite, I'll say that. Aged, poor soul. Spotless clean though, allus was. And I did as she asked, no point doing owt else. But now—'

The gardener stared hard at Bassett and said slowly, with deliberation. 'You think. Robby happy as long as his routine weren't upset. The Mulholland woman a-poking her nose. A welfare person turning up. See? Doesn't take a lot of figuring out. Alice would've been protecting Robby. It could've been an *accident*. And mebbe some of Robby's logs fell atop of him.'

He moved his gaze to straight ahead: a fountain playing. 'If it *were* Alice, I'm a-thinking.'

Two seconds ticked by. 'Or Robby. Needn't have been either of them,' he said sidelong.

Bassett said, 'I'm losing you, Clem.'

'Ar.' The creases on the old gardener's face deepened, and not humorously. 'Can't always make sense of what I'm a-thinking myself,' he said dolefully. 'But I'd been a-weighing a few things up afore that car were found. I never uttered a word about Robby's dad, and if anybody else had a-knowed it wouldn't have stayed a secret all these years, that I do know. Thirteen years between Alice settling in that old place and Edith a-coming from America, twelve years since—and never a whisper? Never in a month of Sundays would it have stayed buried that long if anybody here had a-knowed!

'But I reckon the secret's out now. I reckon somebody in the village *now* knows about it. And I reckon that same somebody's been a-feeding out the odd titbit, the odd piece of information.

'Nothing's been said to me directly—'cepting by the Mulholland woman, and she were a-fishing. But where did she get her bait? Who gave her the maggot to hang on her hook? Nowt I can put a finger on, and mebbe nowt taken seriously. Till now. Word'll soon get round now: Like father, like son.'

Clem flicked his cap at a flying insect preparing to settle on his knee. Watching, Bassett said, 'I've met Alice Meddlar.'

The cap hovered. 'All right, was she?'

'Yes . . .'

The cap took a swipe at the persistent insect. 'Then you know she's a-mellowing. Has her groceries delivered, has the missus from the shop in for a cup of tea every Thursday. Had Kathy McDonald and her little 'un there last Christmas . . . She's getting old, and mebbe she's a-feared of dying alone and unloved. This could spoil things for her.

'And mebbe that's what someone wants,' Clem added a moment later.

Bassett regarded him thoughtfully. 'Were you anywhere near Alice's on Saturday? Did you see a yellow Datsun, or—'

Clem answered before Bassett had finished. Went to a christening in Somerset, he said. His newest granddaughter. 'Fetched me Friday night, brought me back on Sunday.'

Which reply settled in part the question in Bassett's mind. He had thought Clem might be like Tod. Tod had a habit of appearing obtuse while dropping pertinent hints. Might Clem have seen something, been aware of unusual activity near the Meddlar home, for instance, and was reluctant to say so openly? Apparently not.

'Sun's going down, Clem. Best go and give my hens their tea-time corn. Not that they aren't already too fat.' Bassett rose. 'I've enjoyed the talk. Very useful. Did Edith give you her address in America?'

They went to the lodge, where Bassett jotted down the Florida address and telephone number; and names of newcomers to Bletch Heath.

Certain of these stood out: Olivia Mulholland and her sister, Annette Gray; Ken Collier and his wife; Joan and Desmond Arthur, who kept the village shop; and Kathy McDonald.

It was not names Bassett pondered on, however, as he drove from the lodge, it was Clem's *Somebody's been feeding out the odd titbit, the odd piece of information*. *Feeding* implied a deliberate insidious making public Alice Meddlar's terrible secret.

Implied something sinister.

At home, chores done, evening meal cooked, eaten, and cleared away, Bassett settled down at his fireside with pup his companion. He had dialled Directory Inquiries and got

Kathy McDonald's telephone number, which wasn't in the book. Now he considered ringing her up; and Mrs Gray for news of Mrs Mulholland; Edith in America; his friend Jack to ask Jack to find out from gipsy Daniel the truth about Alice Meddlar's husband . . .

But his chair was comfortable, his pipe pleasurable; and anyhow, as Mary might have said had she been here: You're not on the force now (dear), you've retired. Remember?

He did, in spite of himself, write a headline in his notebook, and underneath this, 'Saturday. Clem alibied'; but this was as far as he got. For hadn't he preached to Andy Miller the wisdom of waiting to hear what the head man's wife had to say?

Aye. And hadn't he also asked for Bob Greenaway to give him a tinkle?

At 10.0 p.m., weary of waiting for a telephone call that never came, he and pup took themselves off to bed.

Not as straightforward as someone would have us believe, obviously, Bassett told himself. On this he slept.

CHAPTER 9

It was the following morning, when Bassett was crisping his breakfast bacon, that Inspector Bob Greenaway came on the telephone.

Bob sounded preoccupied. 'This Meddlar, Harry, and McDonald. Andy tells me—or rather, he gained the impression—that you'd like to talk to them before we do. Why?'

'The Meddlar chap's a recluse, doesn't meet people. He's likely to do a runner—'

'He has,' Bob said drily. 'We went to question him early this morning and he took off into the woods like a mad thing. Lost him but we've got his mother. After a tussle. Fought like a wildcat, feet, fists and elbows flying, dozens of them coming at us from every direction. Took a shotgun to us. No damage done, the thing hasn't been fired in ages. Anyway, she's here at the station; been given a sedative and there's a nurse with her. This son of hers . . .' he said hesitantly.

'If he's in the woods you'll never find him, Bob.'

A short silence. Then: 'But you might.'

Another silence, and: 'I can try.'

'Hm.' Bob grunted. 'Rather you than me. He a friend of yours?'

'No—o.'

'OK.' Decision taken, Bob's voice shed its hesitancy. 'As far as I'm concerned he's a loony on the loose with a lethal weapon, a ruddy great axe. I've got men spaced along Cooper's Lane and the area sealed off as best I can, but I'm short on manpower. Want me to organize firearms?'

God forbid! 'Not necessary, Bob.' Fingers crossed. 'Tell your men not to do anything rash.'

'Like approaching him, you mean? Don't worry . . . Hang on, message coming through from Andy, he's there with an incident van . . . Got it. Mrs MacDonald is with him. Says if we leave Robby Meddlar alone he'll return of his own accord . . . And she wants to speak to you.'

'Tell Andy I'm on my way. One thing you could do, Bob—ask Doc McPherson to join us.'

'He's got the 'flu—'

'He'll come,' Bassett said confidently. 'Ask him nicely.'

It took Bassett less than twenty minutes to reach the incident van area. Kathy McDonald, wearing a coat and sensible walking shoes, came to meet him as he got out of his car. One glance at her face dashed a faint hope he'd nursed that she might know Robby's whereabouts.

'Hello.' He greeted her warmly. 'I was hoping Robby might have run to you.'

'I wish he had,' she said wretchedly. 'Hello, pup.' She fondled the labrador for a few seconds through the open window. Then to Bassett: 'I'm glad you are here. I know who you are now.'

'Oh dear.' Trying to cheer her up.

She gave a laugh but her heart wasn't in it. 'I was at the village hall last night, heard people talking. They've found a body, haven't they? I spoke to Clem, too; or more accurately, he to me. He said I was sure to be questioned because I'm that rarity—a friend of Robby's.' At last a proper smile. 'He also said I would do worse than speak to you first.'

Bassett smiled back. 'Where's your infant?'

'With a neighbour who babysits for me.'

'Time to spare then?' Bassett begged. 'Want to keep pup company, or come with me?'

No offence to pup, but—'Come with you.'

Bassett threw a look towards the incident van. 'Give me five minutes with Sergeant Miller.'

Andy Miller was apologetic. 'Sorry, guvnor, had no choice

but to try for an interview after what Mrs Read told us.'

Bassett waved the apology away. 'You've a job to do. What did she say? That she was requested by Olivia Mulholland to take a look-see at the Meddlars?'

Affirmed. 'Only Mrs Read jollied her husband into doing it instead. Actually he was supposed to have a chat with yon Mrs McDonald first, but she was out all day Saturday.'

They left it there for now.

Bassett declined the offer of back-up. 'I'll start from the house, work my way through the woods from there. I'll be taking Kathy McDonald with me, so spread the word. No panic moves. No bawling. If there's any bawling and shouting to be done—I'll be doing it.'

Andy's genial face split in two with a grin. 'Shout and we'll come running, pronto.'

'Cheeky young blighter,' Bassett retorted, departing. He stuck his head back inside the van. 'Keep an eye on my dog for me? Water and bowl down by the front seat.'

'Right-o, Mrs McDonald—'

'Kathy, *please*.'

'Right-o, Kathy. We'll walk up the track, if that is all right with you. Talk as we go, shorten the journey. Tell me about yourself, how you came to be friends with Robby. Are you a relation?'

No, she was no relation, Kathy said. Nor had she heard of the Meddlars, she met them purely by accident.

'My husband Mike is in Qatar, he's an engineer. A highly-paid contract job is about the best chance we have of getting enough money together to put a deposit on a house. We'll be able to join him when he's done a year out there, but in the meantime Mike's uncle offered me Forge Cottage and I jumped at the offer.

'Of course I got myself lost, didn't I? I'd remembered I had to turn right at the church, but after driving for ages along empty lanes it dawned on me I had the *wrong* church.

I pulled in to a lay-by—the one where the Datsun was found—and spotted a van up ahead come from nowhere. I knew it had to have come from *some*where—and the somewhere should be able to direct me. I went looking, and found Robby.'

'Did you drive up?' Bassett slowed his pace to match Kathy's: she was taking two steps to his one.

'Yes.' She described Robby emerging from a barn carrying a bundle of holly. Hens, a cat, Christmas carols on a radio. It had seemed—jolly. Robby hadn't said anything but he had been kind, led her and the baby indoors, sat them by the fire, and had gone upstairs to fetch his mother who was having a nap.

He hadn't run away. 'He must have liked you on sight,' Bassett observed.

'Not me exactly,' Kathy said modestly.

'Your baby?'

'No.' They looked at each other sidelong. 'They have a painting on a wall of Mary and Baby Jesus. And it *was* Christmas, I *was* wearing a blue hooded coat, and I *did* have a baby in my arms,' Kathy said meaningfully.

'Ah!' Bassett visualized her: all smiles, she and the baby all innocence, no threat to Robby. He acknowledged the sentiment in her eyes, looked down at where he was walking. 'You were invited to stay.'

'No room at the inn?' Kathy said, with a trace of yesterday's impishness. 'No. I had taken it for granted that if I booked the electricity to be turned on in the cottage one day it would be done the next. In fact they required three working days' notice, and the holiday intervened, which meant I had to wait a week. As luck would have it I had taken Alice into town with me; she promptly insisted we spend Christmas with her and Robby.'

She confessed she hadn't been over-enthusiastic. At first sight the house had been daunting: heavy dark furniture, dim lighting, old-fashioned atmosphere . . . Alice wearing boots in the house, the man country-shy. 'I was quite wrong. The house turned out to be lovely, and the week really enjoyable. I wrote Mike a ten-page letter about it.'

'You didn't notice anything queer in their, say, behaviour?' Bassett sent her a smile. 'I regret the question, but needs must.'

'You mean did they seem normal?' Kathy said astutely. 'Yes, they did. Eccentric, yes. I had a schoolfriend whose parents were slightly dotty; we girls positively adored them.'

'Any sign of violence? Anything that worried you? That you've thought about since and been disturbed by?'

'No.' Second thoughts. 'Save for—well, Robby's future when Alice passes on. She is very old, when all is said and done. I spoke to her about it once, after Mrs Mulholland had been to see me. Alice said she had family who would watch out for him. She had begun to worry about it herself, she said; but one of the family came to see her now occasionally, she could rely on him. I've not seen this relation, so I've a sneaking suspicion it's not true.'

'Oh, I don't know, it could be,' Bassett said. Daniel Smith's family would never let one of their own, however distantly related, come to grief. 'You saw no irrational behaviour, sudden black moods or temper?'

'No!' Kathy replied with half-laughing impatience. 'They're gentle, kind people, who want to live their own lives.'

They were both puffing a little from the uphill plod. 'Weaklings, aren't we?' Kathy said cheerfully, making small amends for her outburst. 'We worry about Robby but he's probably fitter physically than any of us.'

Bassett gave her a profile wink. 'We're nearly there. House in sight.'

Arrived. The house and yard appeared deserted. No cat. No hens. No sound. Until—Kathy halted, her face lighting up. 'Listen!' Music. 'That's Robby playing the harmonium.'

She pressed Bassett's arm. 'Come on. I'll bet those police-men bulldozed him, frightened him half to death.'

They entered a huge airy kitchen lined with floor-to-ceiling cupboards. Kathy pointed out a ledge under the sink. 'That's where Alice kept the shotgun. The police will have taken it, won't they? She never used it, they'll soon find that out.'

The music ceased. 'Robby's heard us.' She smiled, sig-nalled: This way!—and led Bassett through to a spacious living-cum-drawing-room.

Robby Meddlar—or whoever had been playing the har-monium—had vanished.

'He might be in there.' Kathy pointed to the curtained door in a recess, but stopped Bassett with a look when he moved towards it. 'It's Robby's private room, his retreat.'

'Can you get him out?'

Her eyes flashed a yes. She went to the door and called softly, 'Robby! it's me, Kathy. Will you come out? I've brought a friend of mine to meet you.' To Bassett: 'He'll come when he's ready. He's shy.'

Bassett didn't argue.

He looked round appreciatively: he was no antique expert yet he knew instinctively that he was looking at the equiva-lent of a small fortune. 'It is nice, isn't it?' Kathy said, catching his eye. 'Once I'd got used to it.' She turned a slow full circle gazing at paintings, porcelain, furniture, a beautiful clock. 'You can understand why Alice kept a shotgun. She never *killed* anything with it, not a rabbit or a bird or anything.'

She went to the curtained door again. 'Robby! We can't wait much longer. Please come and say hello!'

To Bassett: 'Alice told me that her late husband was a man of standing, a man of property and wealth.'

'Did she tell you how he died?'

Kathy shook her head. 'Some terrible accident. She didn't tell me what.'

There was an envelope on the mantelshelf propped up against a china dog. 'Do you think Alice would mind?' Bassett said, reaching for the envelope anyway. It wasn't an official envelope but might nevertheless contain a letter from Philip Read advising of his proposed visit. It did not. The letter was from Mottram and Son, Antiques.

Bassett read aloud: 'Dear Alice, delighted to hear from you . . . If the scent bottles and decanters are those I saw last year I think we may be talking about a figure in the region of five thousand pounds . . . Sovereigns, as you know, are priced on the day's value of gold, which is riding high at the present time. I look forward to seeing you on Friday. I shall be in all day. Yours et cetera, Alec.'

He looked at Kathy. 'Friday. That's tomorrow.'

Kathy nodded. 'When she runs out of cash Alice sells something.'

Bassett read the letter once more, restored letter and envelope to the mantelshelf. 'No telephone,' he said. 'Where does Alice keep her other correspondence?'

Kathy waved a hand towards the mantelshelf. 'There. She doesn't receive much.'

'No, I suppose not.'

They both shrugged shoulders and smiled.

A door at the far end of the room was open showing the foot of the stairs. 'Might he have gone upstairs?' Bassett said. He didn't wait for a reply. 'You stay here, Kathy.'

The door also led to what should have been a dining-room or library but resembled a junk room . . . and back to the kitchen, cold store, pantry, scullery. A quick inspection of these showed Bassett nothing.

Upstairs, a wide landing and four doors. Bassett steadied his hand, had shoulders braced and a smile on his face as he gripped the first doorknob . . . Guest bedroom; Kathy's when she stayed here, he guessed, for a large drawer lined with a fleecy blanket stood on a luggage table beside the bed: the baby's 'cot'. His search was quick, clean, methodical: fruitless.

The next room had to be Alice's. A large bedroom. Old-fashioned wooden bed with carved headboard. Faded, once beautiful quilted silk covers. Chinese rugs. Rich mahogany wardrobes, miles of 'em, crammed with clothes, shoes, bags, wigs, all not unpleasantly perfumed . . . Trunks and chests: none containing blankets. Dressing-table overloaded with scent bottles, jewellery and pin boxes, combs and hairbrushes; and in a drawer a collection of photographs, letters of uncertain dates, dog-eared souvenir programmes of various events. Plus, wait, newspaper cuttings.

Newspaper cuttings a quarter of a century old. And this photograph . . . He turned the photograph over, read the message on the back; it was to a young Alice from her then husband-to-be. Remarkable-looking man. He selected two more—intriguing—photographs, put all three and the newspaper cuttings in his inside pocket, to be returned to Alice later.

Robby's room was spartan, the bathroom functional. Nothing there to hold his attention.

'Does Alice drive?' he asked Kathy, joining her downstairs.

'No.'

'Sure?'

'Quite sure.'

'Were you here last weekend?'

'Here?'

'Mm. Come for tea or anything?'

'No.'

'You didn't see Robby on Saturday?'

A headshake.

'Nor Sunday?'

'No.'

Bassett glanced at his watch. 'I think we've waited long enough. We'll have to fetch Robby out.'

But even as Bassett spoke the curtained door creaked open.

CHAPTER 10

'Look.' Sergeant Andy Miller handed the field glasses to Inspector Bob Greenaway and directed his gaze.

'Where?' Bob growled. 'Can't see anything.'

Andy received the glasses back, swept the woods. 'Gone. Bassett and another man. Going walkies.'

'The Meddlar bloke?' Bob Greenaway tried again; again the field glasses gave him nothing. 'Walkies or not,' he grouched, 'I'll give him ten more minutes.'

Andy grinned. He had found them again: two figures sitting side by side on a toppled tree-trunk seemingly immersed in conversation. 'I think you can call off the lads, Bob. They've just been made redundant.'

'Does that include me?' Doc McPherson asked. He stayed, all the same: if Bassett had wanted him there it must be for good reason.

Bob Greenaway's ten minutes stretched to twenty. When finally Bassett showed up at the incident van he was alone. 'He's ready to meet you.' He addressed Bob and Andy together. 'You can't just take him in like any other suspect, you know. He's like a creature of the wild, territorial yet all the same free. Be cruel to bung him in a cage.'

'You don't think he did it,' Andy said bluntly.

Bassett grimaced. 'I didn't say that, Andy. Frankly, I don't think he did. He's slow, backward, but no imbecile. He's strong, very strong, he lugs tree-trunks from the woods on his shoulders—but he says he never hurt anything in his life and I'm inclined to believe him. I'm no expert in the field of mental health, though. Which is why I wanted you here, Jim.' Bassett turned to his white-haired, overcoated doctor friend.

'I'm no psychiatrist either,' Doc said.

'But you are a doctor, Jim.' Bassett sighed. 'Call me an idiot if you like, but the man has lived here, no trouble to anyone as far as I can make out, for twenty-five years. Harmless, Jim. Him and his mother. Local characters, recluses. Figures of fun, no doubt, on occasion; but not violent. If he did it we have to know *why* he did it, what caused him to break out; if he didn't—' He broke off, temporarily at a loss for words.

'Bassett's right,' Doc advised Bob Greenaway. 'If he's a schizophrenic, for example, the worst thing we could do would be to lock him in a cell.'

'And the worst thing I could do would be to leave him on the loose,' Bob argued forcefully. 'He and his mother are prime suspects in a brutal murder case, for God's sake! There's sufficient circumstantial evidence against them to—'

Bassett interrupted. 'I understand that,' he said with quiet emphasis. 'All I'm saying—'

Doc cut in. 'I think I understand what Bassett's saying, Bob. He wants you to bend a few rules. For what it's worth until I've spoken to him, I have a friend who owns a private clinic. A psychiatric clinic.'

'And I can give you the elements of doubt you'll want to satisfy your chief,' Bassett assured Bob.

The Inspector stared, at one then the other. 'OK. But I'm promising nothing until I've seen him. Come on, let's go . . . Want me to be a bloody social worker.' He glared at Andy Miller, who replied facetiously, 'I shouldn't think so, Bob. Look what happens to them.'

'What is this circumstantial evidence?' Doc inquired as they set off for the house.

Bob Greenaway explained that according to the dead man's wife a Mrs Mulholland, who had recently come to live in Bletch Heath, was unhappy about Robby's not mixing in the community. She had wanted Mrs Read to help her rectify this; to which end Mrs Read had come to see Mrs Mulholland last Tuesday, whereupon Mrs M promptly changed her story and told Mrs Read that she thought Robby Meddlar could be dangerous. A whisper she had picked up about Robby's father. Mrs Read had asked Mrs Mulholland's sister what it was all about, and the sister said that in her opinion Mrs Mulholland had been the victim of a joke.

All right, fine, forget the dangerous bit, thought Mrs Read; humour Mrs Mulholland regarding the other. Robby couldn't be compelled to do anything against his wishes, but they could have a chat with his mother, supply her with information and leaflets to study, et cetera.

Not unnaturally, Mrs Read discussed the issue with her husband Philip, who had experience with difficult children and childlike minds. Philip subsequently volunteered to do the visiting.

'We believe he came on Saturday,' Bob said. 'And Mrs Read's reaction when we informed her that Mr Read had been murdered—and where—was: "Olivia was right all along, the Meddlar man is dangerous."'

A natural reaction in the circumstances, Bassett thought. He didn't say so. 'Why Saturday, Bob?'

'Because of the doll.'

Apparently Philip Read had bought the doll for his wife. She had shopped in Glevebourne after having tea with Olivia Mulholland last Tuesday, seen the doll, fallen in love with it, enthused about it at length to her husband. 'Birthday coming up,' Bob explained; 'she knew that if she dropped enough fat hints hubby would buy it for her. Which he did—we checked with the shop-owner late last night. One of those new shops in the mews, specializes in nostalgia.'

A china doll, Victorian dress, all maroon velvet and lace, with straw boater and ribbons.

'Shopkeeper remembers Read.' Andy Miller took up where Bob left off. 'He places him in the shop at just after nine-thirty on Saturday morning. Also, a yellow Datsun, could have been Read's, passed houses adjacent to the war memorial at Bletch Heath a minute or two before ten o'clock. Makes it a fair assumption that he was on his way to the lay-by, more specifically to the Meddlar house: kill two birds with one stone—buy the doll and dispose of his duty call on the Meddlars.'

Bob came in again. 'Mrs Read did say that the idea was for her husband to visit Mrs McDonald first, but Andy asked her about that this morning—'

Andy: 'Mrs McDonald says she was out all day on Saturday. If Read did go to her house he wouldn't have found her in.'

'No proof that he got as far as the Meddlar place, of course,' Bob continued, 'but we think he did. We think he went straight there after leaving Glevebourne. The timings fit. They fit in reasonably well with his eating habits, too. Doc here tells us he died shortly after drinking coffee and eating a digestive biscuit. It's a fact that Read never ate breakfast but invariably had a roll or biscuits at between ten and ten-thirty a.m., in the office and when at home. If he followed the same pattern on Saturday we could be looking at between ten and eleven a.m. as time of death. We think he drew in to the lay-by and had a drink and a biscuit before tackling the Meddlars. There, for his pains, he was whacked across the face and head.'

'Blunt instrument,' Doc said. 'Hit with considerable force. More details I may be able to tell you tomorrow.'

'Blunt instrument, considerable force,' Bob Greenaway repeated. 'Not, I think, the work of an old lady Mrs Meddlar's age. Nor would an old lady have been able to dig that grave. But she could have aided and abetted her son . . . We're here.'

Kathy McDonald appeared at the door as they drove into the yard. Her eyes sent anxious messages to Bassett. 'It won't require all four of us, will it?' he said to no one in particular. 'Don't want to scare the pants off the chap.' He caught Kathy's look of gratitude.

'I'd like you to stay, Mrs McDonald,' Bob said. 'You, Doc. Me—'

'I'll keep Bassett company out here.' Andy turned to Bassett. 'If it's all right with you.'

'All right with me, Andy.'

'Read's car keys, Andy. Briefcase.'

'Still missing.'

'So; those doubts I have,' Bassett said. 'Let's try them out for size.'

He drew Andy to the edge of the yard, pointed to the track. 'You can't see the Meddlar house from the lane; for all you know it's a mile along this track. Who would walk it? Assume not Philip Read. He drank coffee, ate a biscuit, drove up here as we just did. Got out of his car, walked up to the house.

'Until we have a description of the murder weapon we'd be wasting our time reasoning out how he met his death. We'll jump the gap. Someone killed him. He is dead . . . Who shifted the Datsun to the lay-by? Not Alice, Kathy McDonald says Alice doesn't drive. Believe it; if she had been a driver she would have owned a car—far easier to be a recluse if you have your own transport. Kathy McDonald? Unlikely. Kathy wouldn't have left the Datsun in the lay-by, she would have driven it to a spot well away from here.

'Could Robby and his mother have moved the Datsun by manhandling it? Waited until dark, then pushed the Datsun down the track? Possible—you can do anything if you are desperate enough; but could they have put it in neutral and manœuvred it so *neatly* into the lay-by? Again, unlikely . . . Any comment so far?'

Andy said no.

'Try the alternative,' Bassett said. 'Philip Read leaves his car in the lay-by and walks up the track. Is killed. The killer goes through the man's pockets, leaves wallet and identity papers intact but *removes* the car keys.

'Why would Alice or Robby Meddlar want the keys? True, Alice would have realized he must have come in a car. It's possible she might have thought he had a colleague waiting in the car—she could take the keys to the colleague, spin a yarn about Read staying for a while, would the colleague like to go and come back later. On the other hand, let's assume the keys were taken for the sole purpose of gaining entry to the car. For what reason? Certainly not to steal the vehicle.'

'To steal the briefcase,' Andy suggested. 'Mrs Meddlar, thinking there might be papers inside bearing their name.'

'Wouldn't Read have been *carrying* the briefcase, Andy? His badge of office. Containing brochures and forms for Alice should she prove to be receptive? He might have been warned that she could be difficult, didn't care for The Authorities, but would he pander to that? He wore a business suit: why leave his briefcase in the car?

'And what did the killer do with the briefcase? Burn the contents, maybe. The briefcase itself? Why not bury it with the body?'

'I'll bite,' said Andy. 'Why were the keys taken?'

'I don't know,' Bassett confessed. 'I'm not trying to be clever, Andy, I'm trying to make sense of it. I think the killer took the keys in order to steal the doll . . . Consider that. Philip Read wouldn't have been carrying the doll, for heaven's sake. If he drove up, and his car was here in the yard, how did the car get back to the lay-by? If he walked up, *the killer would have had to go to the lay-by*. Who? Say Alice. Say she went to the car, for whatever purpose, and took the doll. If she stole it for herself it should be on a chair in her bedroom, or on the sofa where she would be able to see it, perhaps worship it a little. It isn't. Robby? I can't envisage Robby even touching the car. I doubt if it would have entered his head.'

They had been ambling round the yard as they talked; had arrived at the woodshed, whose door seemed to be permanently propped open. Bassett had already peeped inside on his way down to the incident van after his meeting with Robby. Now he and Andy stood on the threshold and looked hard at what was in there. Logs had been stacked high and graded to size: small, medium, large; chopped firewood, twigs and other kindling sat in tidy heaps on a well-swept cobbled floor. 'So well swept you could eat off it,' Andy remarked. 'Shows he's a *bit* of a nutter.'

Two steps over the threshold and they were staring at a row of axes and axe-heads, saws, tools, a variety of old-fashioned farm implements; a frightening array of points and cutting edges decorated the walls.

'*Robby Meddlar's.*' Andy was amazed.

'Thought-provoking, isn't it?' Bassett said. 'His mother obviously doesn't believe he's dangerous. Let us consider that now, Andy. From what I saw of the dead man's injuries someone had taken a good old swipe at his head and face. Where? Say here. Say the social worker came to the woodshed door—what would Robby have done? We know he's shy, he runs. Meaning he gets out of sight. The furthest he would be able to go would be the corner there, by the saw-horse. What would he have most readily to hand?—an axe or saw. Say he held it defensively, or even simply *looked* at it—would Read have kept coming? I think not. Mrs Read's immediate reaction when she heard of her husband's death was to say, "He *is* dangerous, then." Suggests to me that she would have preached caution to her husband, if only half in jest. Be careful, love!

'Supposing she didn't, though,' Bassett continued. 'I've met Robby, I don't think he's violent—but I'd watch myself, for all that. I'd think twice before going any further than we are now. And I'd leave myself an escape route.

'Anyhow—a swipe, Andy. Hardly room in here to take a swipe.

'Outside then. Robby comes out of the woodshed, the house, chicken barn or wherever—and wallops the social worker. Why? It's against his nature even to have approached Read, a stranger—'

'The woods,' said Andy. 'Someone told Read he'd find Robby in the woods. He pussy-footed, startling Robby— Robby swings round and clonks him one.'

'With his axe?' Bassett said. 'If Read's injuries were made by an axe I'm a Dutchman. And what next, eh, Andy? Having killed him, he pops home for a blanket to wrap him in?'

'He'd have had to pop home for a spade,' Andy said.

They moved out into sunshine, watched the cat slinking along the shed wall to check its dish just inside the woodshed, and go on to a favourite sunning position.

'Pity Doc can't be more specific about the murder weapon,' Bassett said. ''Flu slowed him down, I suppose . . . Bob got a search warrant, Andy?'

'Yes, and it'll take a week to do this lot. The house, grounds, outbuildings,' the Sergeant complained.

Bassett nodded sympathetically. Andy followed his thoughtful gaze to a point beyond the trees overlooking the lane, watched him glance round at the house, scan the yard, look at the shed and up at the woods; and saw now the gleam in Bassett's eyes. Cogs working: what had he thought of? Something to do with the blanket? The spade?

No, no. Something else.

'Tell them to start with the woodshed, Andy. For all I've just said, I think that's where you might find the murder weapon.'

Small sounds of fuss came from within the house. Doc McPherson was the first to emerge, his nose red from over-use of his handkerchief, his shoulders a shade more stooped than usual; but he smiled and shrugged genially as he joined Bassett, Andy having gone to find Bob. 'Robby seems pretty right to me. They are taking him in, though, Harry. Wise, I think, to practise caution.'

As Kathy appeared Doc made eyes at Bassett. 'I'll do what I can and be in touch.' He went on to the police car.

Kathy ran up to Bassett. 'Robby has to go with them.'

'I know,' he said kindly.

Tears surfaced, she blinked them away angrily. 'Mustn't cry,' she sniffed, laughing. 'The doctor is going to get special treatment for him. He didn't kill that man, you know. Will you find out who really did do it?'

'That I shall certainly do,' Bassett promised.

He looked at the black hair flowing freely today, the concerned blue eyes, the mouth whose corners moved naturally upwards although she was distressed, and he couldn't resist giving her a fatherly hug. No urchin's scent of damp bark and wild thyme today, today's perfume was out of a bottle. Nice, but he thought the other suited her better. He let her go. 'Robby's coming. I'm glad; he's looking far from miserable.'

'You're looking forward to it, aren't you, Robby?' Kathy said as they all met. 'Meet new people, see new places.'

Robby proudly showed off his suitcase. 'My mother said she would have to go away one day, and I'd go somewhere else to live. She said there would be trees, just like here.' It was as much as he ever spoke at any one time.

'Remember what I told you.' Bassett winked encouragement. 'There might be some things you won't like, but treat it all as an adventure.'

'Adventure. Yes.'

Bob Greenaway was the last to leave the house. He waited until Kathy was escorting Robby to the car before addressing Bassett. 'He insists he didn't hit Read, didn't see his mother or anybody else hit him. OK, maybe he didn't strike the blow—but I'm damned sure he buried him. I'll stake my summer holiday on it.'

'I won't argue with that, Bob.' Bassett spoke to himself, Bob hadn't waited to hear his response.

Andy Miller, driving, sent him a short friendly blast on the horn as the police car slid off towards the track.

Hang on! What about me!

It figured. They had left him to walk down.

CHAPTER 11

'No, no message, thank you, Jilly. I'll try later.'

Bassett put down the telephone. He had been trying to get hold of Jack the Poacher to tell him what had happened, but Jack and his wife had gone out. He now toyed with the idea of telephoning gipsy Daniel Smith directly, but he knew from past experience Daniel's dislike of telephones; they would probably end up talking to one another through a third party, never very satisfactory. No matter. He brewed himself a mug of tea and took it out into the garden.

Pup was treading her boundaries sniffing out news, as dogs do; Gert and Daisy, his wayward hens, were busy attempting to tunnel out of the hen run, aerial escape having been blocked by the higher wire-netting; Cocky patrolled majestically. Good; all as normal. The fox appeared to have been thwarted.

Being entertained by the antics of his chickens was a favourite pastime, they reminded Bassett so of people; soon, however, he forgot their clucking, forgot the charm of treetop birdsong, the minute sounds of life going on all around him, and thought of Robby.

My mother said she would have to go away one day, and I'd have to go somewhere else to live.

When had she said it?

He thought of Clem's words—that Robby was happy as long as his routine wasn't upset. Today Robby's routine *had* been upset, with no bad result. Had Alice since that years-ago conversation with Clem, prepared Robby for the change that would come when she died? 'I'm growing old, Robby. One day I won't be here any more . . .'

Or had she said it recently?

Since Saturday, for instance.

In his mind's eye Bassett re-read the letter from the antique dealer, Alec Mottram. Alice Meddlar had scent bottles and decanters to sell. And she must have sold items before, Bassett told himself, therefore there was nothing extraordinary about the contents of the letter . . . Or should he be considering *fleeing* money? There was just time for Alice to have written to the antique dealer after Philip Read's death on Saturday, and to have received the reply, postmarked Tuesday.

Although . . . *fleeing* money; *urgency*. Wouldn't urgency have had the woman waiting on Mottram's doorstep first thing on Monday morning?

His mind's eye picked out the beginning and the end of the letter. *Dear Alice . . . Yours, Alec*. They were on Christian name terms. Meaning that Mr Mottram might be able to supply some answers.

Bassett returned to the house, picked up the telephone.

Alec Mottram was small, balding, at a guess in his sixties, and, as Tod Arkwright might say, clearly worth a bob or two.

Yes, he had received a letter from Mrs Meddlar on Monday, he said, replying to Bassett's first question. He had answered the letter immediately, she was a valued client of long standing.

'Do you actually buy her stuff?' Bassett inquired. 'Or sell them on commission?'

'Commission usually. More often than not in Alice's case I send them to auction, she has such interesting items.'

'The items mentioned in the letter, would they have gone to auction?'

'Oh yes, most assuredly. May I ask why you wish to know? You said on the telephone that you were a friend of Alice's . . .'

'In fact I'm a friend of a friend,' Bassett said. 'Mrs

Meddlar is in a spot of trouble. I thought she might have wanted ready cash rather urgently.'

'Oh, I *see*.' The small puzzled frown vanished. 'Well, if she lets me have the items I'll be glad to let her have something on account,' the antique dealer said generously. 'She should know that.'

'Did she mention urgency in her letter to you, Mr Mottram?'

'Not at all.' He was vaguely mystified. 'It was a perfectly routine letter, I thought.'

'How well do you know her?' Bassett's tone invited confidence.

'I've known her for a very long time, but I can't say I know her well.'

'This shop is fairly new,' Bassett said. 'You haven't been in Glevebourne long?'

'No. We have another shop near Leominster, which I leave in the capable hands of my daughter.' The frown was threatening to return.

'Leominster is where your association with Alice Meddlar began?'

'Yes.'

'When her husband was alive?'

'Yes, but—'

'You knew Alice's husband?'

'Yes.'

'Ah! thank heavens.' Bassett feigned a sigh of relief. 'I was beginning to think he was fictitious. Is there somewhere we might go to talk?' The shop was empty of customers but might not remain so.

'Who are you?' Alec Mottram demurred. 'A solicitor?'

Bassett decided to be frank. 'I'm a retired policeman, Mr Mottram. A man has been found murdered on land next door to the Meddlar property, and at the moment evidence is piling up against her and her son. Means, a possible motive, opportunity. As they have lived a reclusive existence for a number of years, they are not in a good position to defend themselves.'

With frankness had come geniality. The antique dealer bolted the shop door, lowered the blind. It was his early-closing day anyway and lunch-time was less than an hour from now. 'If you'd like to come through—'

To a room at the back, pleasantly furnished and boasting a drinks cabinet. 'Take a pew. If you were Alice I'd be offering you a sherry. Would you like something stronger? I'm going to have a whisky myself.'

'I'll keep you company. A small one, thank you.' Bassett smiled.

'What rank did you retire with?' Alec Mottram asked, breaking the seal on a bottle.

'Detective Chief Superintendent.'

'Alice is lucky to have you on her side.'

'I'm on the side of justice,' Bassett said. 'If they didn't do it, someone else did . . . There is a faint possibility of a link with the past—her husband; which I'm sure you know is a touchy subject with Alice.'

The other nodded. 'She's always been a funny one over it.' His smile was amused and kind. 'Hot and bothered when I told her I was opening a shop in Glevebourne. Made me promise never to mention Peter to anyone.' He aped Alice: 'No one knows, no one must ever know, you promise me now.' He changed his voice, 'I think you know who he was already, so I'm not breaking my word.'

Bassett metaphorically patted the newspaper cuttings in his pocket. 'The Hereford Hammer.'

'The Gipsy Champion. Unbeatable in his time.'

'A boxer.'

'No way.' Alec Mottram chuckled. 'Boxers abide by the Marquis of Queensberry Rules. The Hammer was a prizefighter. Bare knuckles, no rules. The fight would continue until a boxer could no longer toe the line. You know what I mean by that? Rounds could last up to five minutes

unless there was a knock down. There was no count. They'd
take the break. As long as both men could stand at the line
facing each other at the beginning of the next round the
fight would continue. I've known them go fifty-two rounds
to win the prize. Each fighter would put up a purse, whatever
he and his mates could afford; the opponent would match
it. Winner took all. Then of course there would be the bets.

'It was how I came to be interested in antiques and
precious metals—following the fancy, going with the win-
ners to exchange cash winnings for gold. Gold chains, gold
sovereigns, anything made of solid gold. I was a bit of a lad
in those days, in my early twenties, few years after the war.'

Bassett grinned. 'Bit of a lad' now, given half a chance,
if his expression was anything to go by.

But he'd met Pete Meddlar before that, the antique dealer
told him. 'My father owned hop fields. Used to be hop fields
all over at one time. All round here, Glevebourne included;
did you know that? As a kid I used to love hop-picking time,
watching the gipsies arrive, whole families, the same year
after year when they were right workers, mean good workers.
I remember—I'd be about six—getting up at dawn and
sneaking off to where they were camped. They'd be at their
fires, breakfasts sizzling on—not frying pans but spades.
Eggs, bacon, sausages—and potatoes baked round the hot
coals. Smelt delicious! Made my mouth water, I can tell
you . . . Then I started sneaking down at other times, and
that was when I first saw Peter. He'd be twelve or thirteen.
Used to fight then. With other lads and some of the men.

'I met up with him again after the war, as I said. How it
came about isn't important; one of my many and nefarious
pursuits. We went all over the country to see him fight. The
Hereford Hammer was King. Go on! give him a hammering,
Peter! Sounds vicious now, when you think about it. But
fortunes could be won and lost. I've seen men bet a thousand
pounds a time—big money in those days. And lose as
much.'

'All illegal, of course.'

A nod. 'The illegality added to the excitement. We always had to be one step ahead of the police. Like today's Acid Parties. The police knew the fights went on, but catching them at it was another matter. They would turn up when it was all over, the following day sometimes. I've run with the best at the sight of a policeman's helmet. We could empty a field in seconds. I dare say it still goes on. In fact I know it does; but don't ask me for details, I haven't any. I quit the scene longer ago than I care to remember.'

'After Peter Meddlar killed a man, in fact.'

Another nod. 'An accident, of course. But the fight being illegal, Peter went down for manslaughter. Was the end of Pete too, really. Knocked the stuffing out of him. Not the manslaughter charge, he gave himself up; the taking of another life. Terrible to see him, this big hard man changed overnight into a nothing. He went clean out of his mind and died in a prison hospital.'

'How did he meet Alice, a lady's maid?'

'At a wedding. He'd never bothered with women before. Along came Alice and that was it. Often the case, isn't it? Big tough men fall for dainty women. She was a slip of a thing. And so ladylike. He was a rich man by then, mind. Bought her a house at Leamington Spa in Warwickshire. Her idea. She wanted a house, and she wanted it where he wouldn't be known; they lived quietly there for part of the year, travelled for the remainder, to horse fairs and so on. Peter still boxed when the purse was good.'

'Robby went with them?' Bassett said.

'Goodness, yes. They'd been married a number of years before Robby arrived. Pete was the proud father, showed his son off to everybody.'

'Did you see much of Robby, Mr Mottram?'

'Not after Alice moved to Bletch Heath. She would bring him once or twice a year to Leominster, until he grew up. He preferred to stay at home after that. Why do you ask?'

'I wondered if you could tell me how handicapped he is.'

'Oh . . . I couldn't say.' The antique dealer shook his head. 'Alice did once tell me he would always be mentally immature, they had suggested she put him in a home. She wouldn't hear of it. He was happy where he was, with her. He had fresh air and freedom—I think she was thinking of his gipsy blood and the boy needing fresh air and space around him, which couldn't be guaranteed in an institution. Also she was determined to bring him up to love nature and be gentle. Again, thinking of his dad, I suppose. Wanted to be sure the boy never got a hankering to box . . . Is that how this man they've found died? A blow?'

Bassett nodded: yes. 'But not with a fist. The man his dad fought—'

'Chap from Newcastle-on-Tyne. Big as himself. They'd fought before.'

'Mm. I was going to ask if there was any possibility of a relation, his grown-up children perhaps, seeking revenge even after this length of time.'

'Very unlikely. Everybody knew the dangers. If a man got hurt, well, it was one of those things. I never heard of anyone bearing a grudge. In fact, the family of the man Pete killed were sure to have been among Pete's supporters in the courtroom.'

'Why did Alice cut herself off?'

'I don't believe she did completely. She used to come and see me.'

'How did she get to you? Did she drive?'

'She didn't drive. Bus, years ago,' the antique dealer replied. 'Taxi after they started taking buses off the road. And the visits became fewer as they became more expensive and Alice infirm . . . She certainly turned her back on the gipsies and travellers though, I grant you that. Again, because of Robby. You know children—the others would have had him sticking his fists up. Come on, show us! Show us you're like your dad! Or else tease him when he couldn't

fight. Bah! Go on, you're no son of the Hereford Hammer!
Kids can be very cruel. Alice was determined he wouldn't
fight. Let's be honest, to be as good as The Hammer you've
got to be hard. And ruthless.'

'One more question, Mr Mottram,' Bassett said. 'Do you
know of an Olivia Mulholland or Annette Gray? Or a man
named Ken Collier, wears his hair in a plait?'

No. No to all of them.

'I take it Alice won't be keeping her date with me
tomorrow?'—as Bassett drained his glass and made to
rise.

'It's doubtful.'

'Well, if there's anything I can do. I'd be obliged anyway
if you would let me know how they fare.'

Bassett shook his hand: firm grip. 'I'll do that.'

From the antique shop to Glevebourne Police Station. For
the desk sergeant a cheerful greeting, and: 'Where do you
keep the photocopier?'

'There—' indicating a door. 'See Julie.'

Blonde Julie was photocopying the last newspaper cutting
when Andy Miller breezed in, and out. 'Andy! Got something for you!' Bassett caught up with Andy at the foot of
the stairs.

'Can only give you a minute, guvnor. Bit of a flap on.'
Hastiness under control.

'A minute is all I want,' Bassett fibbed. 'What flap?'

Andy motioned: they took the stairs to the first floor and
Bob Greenaway's office. On the way Andy told him in
rushed fashion that Alice Meddlar had been taken to hospital, suspected heart attack, and that Bob was bending rules
on Robby Meddlar's behalf and getting stick for it; but by
the time they reached the office—Bob wasn't there—his
speech had reverted from the staccato to normal, and the
old familiar cheeky grin was back.

'What the heck, guvnor. The main problem is having two

suspects you can't eliminate—Mrs Meddlar because she's had a heart attack, and how sane, i.e. reliable is she anyway?—and Robby Meddlar, nothing he says can be taken down and used because he is mentally handicapped, therefore unfit to plead. Can you wonder Bob is ready to tear his hair out?'

Bassett made a face. 'As long as you don't fall into the trap of believing you've got your man and so let other investigations slide.'

He looked at the shotgun in a plastic bag on Bob Greenaway's desk. 'This Alice Meddlar's?'

'The butt could be the blunt instrument.'

It could. Just.

'This something I've got for you, Andy.' Bassett spread the photocopies out on Bob's desk, invariably neat and tidy, Andy's a mess. 'From newspapers twenty-five years ago.' A finger pointed. 'The Hereford Hammer. Peter Meddlar, prizefighter.' Pointed again. 'Killed John O'Connor in an illegal contest. Went down for manslaughter, died in prison. Peter was Alice's husband. Be interesting to know where O'Connor's folks are, if he has any.' The finger moved again. 'Venue, Appleby Horse Fair. Police, Yorkshire. When you have a minute to spare have a word with them. Could be someone still around who remembers the case.'

Andy pored over the cuttings keenly. 'I've heard of these illegal boxing matches.' He looked up. 'What's on your mind, guvnor?'

'Newcomers to Bletch Heath, Andy. A story kept under wraps for twenty-five years which all of a sudden crops up again. I could do with more names.' No O'Connor in Bletch Heath or environs, he'd checked. 'The dead boxer's widow, did she marry again? Did his children, if any, take their stepfather's name? Should we start looking for a son whose name is not O'Connor but something else? Or a married daughter?'

'Revenge?'

'Of a kind. Against the Hammer's wife. Remote; a possibility nevertheless. Stranger things happen.'

Andy agreed it was worth a try. 'Bob should be free at around two o'clock,' he said helpfully.

'He'll have seen enough of me for one day. I'll pop in tomorrow,' Bassett said. 'This afternoon I'm going to visit a couple of ladies.'

To demand from one the telephone number of Olivia Mulholland in Scotland. To ask the other what prompted her to begin delivering groceries to recluse Alice Meddlar.

First, a trip to the Meddlar homestead: to look at a stretch of ground in the yard he wanted to examine more closely. Plus a peep at Robby's private room.

'Private' was intriguing.

CHAPTER 12

The search for incriminating evidence had begun: outside
for the murder weapon, inside the house for the social
worker's fingerprints, the briefcase, the doll, blood on walls,
furniture, floors. So far the only item bagged was an outdoor
jacket of Robby's: spots of what appeared to be blood on
one shoulder. Other clothing was being piled up. 'Some job,
this,' a disembodied voice bellyached. Every door in the
house was open.

Bassett met with no opposition apart from a deferential
reminder not to touch anything, or else to pull on a pair of
those disposable gloves there. 'Brought me own!' He held
them aloft. He'd come prepared.

Robby's private room was clean and tidy, a man's room
yet a boy's room: table, chair, armchair, radio; books,
picture books mainly, and mainly about animals, birds,
nature, and for some reason mythology; paints, crayons,
jigsaw puzzles, a box of toys gathering dust. Nothing to
stir Bassett. His curiosity had been satisfied.

Leaving, he said to the officer who had offered him the
gloves, 'All right if I put some food out for the cat and
give the chickens some corn? Don't want them dying of
starvation, do we?'

The stretch of ground? Only a keenly observant eye would
have seen what Bassett had seen, there were so many tufts
of grass sprouting around the edges of the yard. Tufts on
paths too, weeds sprung up between paving stones. On the
paths someone—Alice or Robby—had taken a spade and
scraped grass off at ground level for much of their lengths.
At the edges of the yard this had been done in one place
only. Seen from the house the gap appeared to be one of
many, from the woodshed that particular patch of earth had

somehow seemed to be too flat. Still did. Had something other than grass been shovelled up from the spot—blood, for instance?

Bassett hadn't drawn attention to it when he was here earlier. Now was the time to do so. Let the team have the credit for it. He went to hunt out the photographer.

'We're closed!' Joan Arthur mouthed this to Bassett through the shop window, whose display of ice-cream and soft-drinks advertisements she was smartening up for the fast advancing tourist season. She was small, pleasant, and she herself in pink and white looked good enough to eat. Bassett had summed her up on a previous visit as a good sort, laughter lines more noticeable than the worry creases between her eyebrows—you had to look for those; and when he mouthed back, 'Won't keep you a minute,' and gestured, 'I'll give you a hand,' the laughter lines increased.

Nuisance, she thought. She had hoped to complete the window uninterrupted, it was three o'clock already, she had wanted some of her half day to herself. But he had such a nice face, like a bloodhound of fond memory, and was so gentlemanly if ever so slightly comical—that hat of his!—oh, never mind! she could finish the window tomorrow.

'I'm supposed to ask for identification, aren't I?' she jollied him as she let him in. Although she knew who he was now, there wasn't much escaped her ears.

'Name's Bassett. I'm assisting the police with their inquiries.'

The words were pompous, the facial expression the opposite; Joan, her better nature having taken the upper hand, might have prolonged the joking had she known him better. Instead she turned the joke on herself. 'Am I to be ticked off about Mrs Meddlar's box of groceries?'

'Good grief, no.'

'Only I did argue a bit strongly when the police prevented me from delivering them. I know they're there because of the body they've found, but—' She stopped. A new thought. 'Alice is all right, is she? She's not ill or anything?'

'She's in hospital. Comfortable at the last bulletin,' Bassett said.

'Hospital? Oh, the poor love.'

Genuine concern? Bassett thought so. Furthermore he doubted that she was a daughter of the dead boxer, John O'Connor; her attitude was wrong. To seek revenge and go through with it after twenty-five years you must have harboured bitterness. This woman's face showed none. Nevertheless . . .

'I've been racking my brains trying to recollect where I've seen you before,' he said, giving her a wide-eyed almost mischievous where-was-it? look.

'Oh, who's to say?' Her laugh had plenty of humour in it. 'Go abroad for your holidays and you're likely to bump into the very neighbours you were glad to be leaving behind for a fortnight. That's happened to us more than once!'

'What was your maiden name?'

'Herbert. I was pleased to change it to Arthur.' Joke there, too. 'We've lived in a fair few places,' she continued. 'Reading, Hove—' trying some out on Bassett. 'Portsmouth?'

Portsmouth. 'I was born a lap away!' he exclaimed truthfully. 'Gosport.'

'That's it!' On target. 'It could be my mother you knew. Gosport is where she comes from, and I'm very like her, everybody says.'

Bassett was sure he didn't know her mother, but within a few minutes he had a potted history of the shop-lady's family—her father had been a Trinity House pilot; and of her husband's—his folks until recently kept a public house; had gleaned that she and husband Desmond had been childhood sweethearts; and—the crux—that both sets of parents were alive, that one set had celebrated their Golden Wedding Anniversary, the others weren't far behind.

Exit Joan or Desmond Arthur being an O'Connor.

Yet a puzzle remained.

'I'm curious,' Bassett said quizzically. 'Mrs Meddlar is by all accounts difficult to get close to, yet you have succeeded. How'd you do it?'

'I'm not that close,' Joan protested mildly.

'You deliver her groceries; she hadn't had them delivered before.' Bassett persisted gently.

'Never put a foot inside the shop. Still doesn't. It just came about, is all I can say. Desmond and I sank every penny we had into this shop after we were made redundant, so we had to make a go of it regardless of people warning us that village shops are on the wane. We advertised— leaflets to every house and a follow-up visit—'

She had called on Alice a day or so after a leaflet had gone into the letter-box. 'I'd have gone right by, didn't realize there was one there to tell the truth, if I hadn't seen the postman stop. And me being dead keen,' she said, voicing enthusiasm. 'The postie said I'd not get an order from her, but I thought nothing venture . . . Anyway, the old love was *grateful*. Calls me Joan now. Brews a pot of tea.'

'You weren't put off by the tales—'

'Bah!' Joan Arthur was impatient of gossips. 'Mr Bassett, I've worked for the general public most of my working life: believe all you're told and you'd go bonkers. I speak as I find. Alice Meddlar was friendly to me from the outset and that's all that bothers me. Anyway, this latest nonsense originates from Cissie Beardmore, and anyone with an atom of sense can see that Cissie's going senile, bless her.'

'Latest nonsense?'

'This tale going round about Robby's dad being a madman, a psycho. Dredged up out of the blue after all this time? Got to be nonsense! Poor Cissie had likely been watching some soap on television when Mrs Mulholland paid her a visit, and got everything mixed up in her head.

In one ear and out the other with most of us. Typical of
Mrs Mulholland to take it as gospel. You'd think with her
experience, so-called, she would know better.'

'Of course she's a newcomer,' Bassett said. 'Mysteries
don't normally exist among villagers who have lived in a
place all their lives—everybody's life is an open book.' He
smiled. 'Strange how outsiders get to know about our vil-
lages when often we're barely on any map. My wife and I
chose Oakleigh during a touring holiday. You, I dare say,
were looking for a village shop—'

'Yes, and we heard about this one from a friend of my
mother's who was evacuated here during the war.'

'Ken Collier and his wife—?'

'Are from over the border, Wales. Ken answered a job
advert for Boon's Farm. But they're Birmingham born, I
think. Mrs Gray comes from Cornwall, that place where
the water supply was poisoned by chemicals; she came here
because of a relation who's in a nursing home. Near where
you live; not Rosemead, the other one. Mrs Gray used to
be a children's nanny, you know. And Mrs Mulholland
came to be with her. She's been all over: the Midlands,
Scotland, Manchester . . . While I think of it—do you know
which hospital Alice is in?'

'I think the Cottage Hospital, Mrs Arthur. I honestly
don't know.' Never occurred to him to ask.

'Never mind, I'll find it.' A smile, a hesitant, 'What about
Robby?'

Bassett assured her that Robby was in good hands. She
was glad. 'Did you see much of him when you took his
mother's groceries?' Bassett asked.

'Not really. He's painfully shy.'

'His mother dotes on him,' Bassett said, eyeing her.

'And the other way round,' Joan said, putting in a word
for Robby. 'Alice couldn't manage without him, she's told
me so herself. Does all the heavy work, keeps the fires going.
Have you seen his woodshed?' She made it sound like a

sight not to be missed. 'I told Des, wish you were that tidy! Mind you, I did think it was an obsession, you know what I mean, Robby being the way he is. I asked him about it once. He didn't answer straight away, he never does, had to take time to think about things. Answered me a week later, poor chap. The answer was so sensible, though, when it did come.' Her voice filled out with praise if not wonderment. 'He said if he always keeps things neat and tidy it means less work in the end, not more. What do you think of that?'

'Not such a daft 'un then, is he?' Bassett said.

A few minutes later he was heading for Annette Gray's house.

'Oh! what luck!' Annette cried, opening the door to him. 'My sister Olivia is on the phone. Would you like a word?'

'I *would*, Mrs Gray. Thank you.' He waited while she spoke to her sister. Then: 'Mrs Mulholland?'

'Mr Bassett. Annette has been telling me about you. And Philip. Dreadful tragedy! I feel responsible, I really do!' She had a strong voice marred by a slight affected whine. 'I understand you want to ask me some questions?'

'If you wouldn't mind. You asked *Mrs* Read to call on Mrs Meddlar, I believe. Did you make any kind of approach yourself?'

'Not directly, no. No, I didn't.'

'Why not? May I inquire?'

'The woman's reputation. One had to tread softly. She had resisted all forms of help for so long one wasn't sure one would make an impression.'

'*Mr* Read—' Bassett began.

'Philip was by far the best person for the job. He had the knowledge and expertise. Wonderful with difficult children. And Robby is a child really, is he not? Philip would have been able to assess the situation, propose recommendations. He would have done *some*thing.'

Bassett winced.

'Did you ever meet Robby Meddlar, Mrs Mulholland?'

'Well, no, not exactly.'

Only saw him peering in at Kathy McDonald's window, eh?

'May I ask who told you about Robby's father?'

'Where does one hear these things, Mr Bassett? The shop, the village hall . . .'

'In effect, then, you acted upon hearsay.'

'Hearsay?' An exasperated short silence ensued. Spare us from a world of dense Bassetts! 'It was, if I may say so, common knowledge, Mr Bassett!'

It wasn't always common knowledge, Bassett longed to retort. It had been Alice Meddlar's secret for a quarter of a century; therein lay the puzzle.

'Mrs Read came to see you last week,' he said. 'Can you remember what she was wearing?'

'What on earth has that to do with anything?'

'Probably nothing, Mrs Mulholland. I'll hand you back to Mrs Gray now. Thank you for your help.' He gave the receiver to Annette, mimed, 'May I wait?' and moved politely along the hall.

There was a second small table there: a folded headsquare, knitted gloves, a small pile of church magazines, a scattering of picture postcards, which Bassett glanced at idly. One caught and held him. The picture was of flower gardens in Cheltenham. He flipped it over. It had been sent to Mrs Mulholland at an old address in Fort William, Scotland, and forwarded on to Bletch Heath; clearly some time ago. The message read: 'Remember me? Eileen (Welling)? Married now and moving to Cheltenham. So happy I have to tell the world! If you are ever down this way give me a ring and we'll have a meal.' The telephone number followed.

Bassett read the card again, saw that Annette had her back to him; slid the card into his pocket.

Seconds later Annette was saying cheerio to her sister. 'Olivia's coming home,' she told him. 'Eileen will need her support.' She rolled her eyes: meaning that Eileen would get it whether she needed it or not. A little laugh came next as she read Bassett's mind. 'I'm not unhappy about it. I may soon have my home to myself. She has a job lined up. A responsible position with a flat thrown in. She's just given me the news.'

'In Scotland?' Being friendly.

'No. She won't give me details but I gather it's fairly local.'

'What about you? You won't mind living alone?'

Annette Gray shook her head, smiling.

'You were a children's nanny, I hear.'

She groaned, laughed. 'Bless Olivia! She tells everyone I used to be a nanny. She has a fixation: my one claim to fame as far as Olivia is concerned. Meet my sister Annette, the famous nanny!'

Bassett laughed with her. 'Famous nanny? Or nanny to someone famous?'

'Neither. I was a nanny for only four years when I was very young, before I married. To a dear little boy named Charlie, whose parents were university professors. They had a gorgeous house on the outskirts of Birmingham. They introduced me—unbeknowns—to my husband. He was a friend of theirs . . . I hardly like to ask, but Philip— have they arrested anyone yet? Olivia wanted to know. Of course I couldn't tell her.'

'No arrest,' Bassett replied. 'Investigations proceeding, as we say. The case isn't as plain sailing as one would have expected.'

'Oh?'

'Mm. Complications.' Bassett uttered it almost throw-away fashion, affecting not to have noticed the sudden dulling of the smile, the faintest flicker of alarm. 'You said your sister went away on Monday,' he said. 'She was here on Saturday?'

'Saturday? Yes, we were both here. Olivia went to the library, and I to the shop. Why do you ask?'

'I wondered if Philip Read had been here.'

'Here to this house? No. I don't think Olivia has ever met the man, to be honest.'

'He hasn't been here at all, ever?'

'No, I'm sure not.' She smiled, said, 'I'll show you out,' as Bassett moved towards the front door.

When they stood on the step, 'Sally's son's house,' Bassett said. 'Is it the one across the road?'

No, they were the Browns. Nice little family. Four boys. 'John's house is round the corner. The first house you come to. There's a swing in the garden.'

'I'll find it. Thank you.'

He didn't go looking for Sally's John. It was the people in the house opposite he wished to speak to. Alas, the woman who opened the door to his thumb on the bellpush was not Mrs Brown.

'I'm the baby-sitter. Mrs Brown won't be home until ten tonight, she's doing a double shift at the Cottage Hospital. Mr Brown will be home around six.'

She had thin blonde hair, an undernourished face, and a bulge at her middle. Bassett hadn't the heart to detain her. He touched his hat. 'Sorry to have troubled you. I'll come again tomorrow, Mrs—?'

'Collier. Megan Collier.'

This village isn't going to die in a hurry, Bassett thought happily, leaving. Mrs Brown had four children. Megan Collier was expecting . . .

Children. Philip Read—was good with difficult children. Robby—childlike. Annette Gray—used to be a children's nanny. Mrs Mulholland—concerned for Kathy and her young Michael. Children everywhere.

From the young to the old, and senility—second childhood. Mm. He decided to stop by and say hello to Cissie
Beardmore before going home to Oakleigh.

And he pondered. Pondered on that tiny niggle at the
back of his mind . . . Something Mrs Mulholland had said.

CHAPTER 13

No sooner was Bassett home than the telephone rang. Jack on the other end of the line. 'You've been trying to get hold of me, Harry.'

'I wanted information about Alice's husband, Jack. Got it now from another source. You've heard about Philip Read's body being found?'

'Yes. How bad is it?'

'Not good. Alice and Robby Meddlar are virtually in custody.'

They talked for several minutes, at the end of which Jack said he would go see Daniel after he'd had a bite to eat. 'Anything you want me to ask him?'

'Yes. See if he knows whether Robby ever had a nanny. Also, are there any relations who stand to benefit from Alice's death or incarceration. There's just a chance that she and Robby have been framed. Don't ask me to explain— I can't. My head's full of cotton wool at the moment. Ideas rushing in with nowhere to go.'

Call ended, Bassett put a lazy—tinned—meat pie in the oven for his tea, gave pup hers, locked his chickens in for the night, then rang up Edith Turner in America. Luck was on his side. The lady was friendly, outgoing, delighted to speak to him—and told him what he wished to know.

'Cissie Beardmore knew the story,' he said later to pup. 'She had known it all along. She had known Alice's married name, read about The Hammer in the newspapers, made the connection but kept the knowledge to herself.' Cissie was like that, the American woman had said. You could tell Cissie anything and she would never gossip it about.

'Until senility overtook her,' Bassett murmured. 'I knew a gent, an upright man, spoke impeccable King's English,

never uttered a swear word in his life. Then senility struck—
he started swearing like a trooper, effing and blinding until,
well, his dear wife daren't take him out in the end. An
incredible personality change!' cocking an eye at pup, who
had dozed off, soothed into slumber by his voice.

The timer on the oven went. Bassett removed his pie, was
slicing through the crust, savouring the delicious aroma
of steak cooked in ale, when Andy Miller came on the
telephone.

'This O'Connor, guvnor. The man Meddlar senior killed
in that fight. I've been on to Yorkshire, I thought the local
cop shop could be my best bet. They put me on to a retired
sergeant who knew all about it. He says O'Connor was
single and an orphan. Had a Gran somewhere but she'd be
long gone by now.'

Exit completely revenge by O'Connor's family.

Andy was still speaking. 'Bob wants to know what's going
on.'

'What I said before, Andy. Newcomers to Bletch Heath.
If perchance one of them had been, say, a son or daughter
of O'Connor's, and discovered Alice living in comparative
luxury while their own mother was struggling . . . A twisted
mind seeking a perverted revenge . . . Since O'Connor has
no family, end of trail.'

'That's it?'

'That's all there is at the moment, Andy. Got to wear me
thinking cap for a bit.'

And finish me pie.

At the station Andy passed on Bassett's explanation to
Bob Greenaway. Doc McPherson was with them. For Doc's
benefit Bob said, 'Philip Read's wife was asked by a Mrs
Mulholland to help her get Robby Meddlar to a Day Centre
or somesuch, improve his life. At the last minute she
changed her mind, came up with a theory that Robby could
be dangerous . . . And I've told this already. Why the hell
am I repeating myself?'

'Because,' Doc said, 'when Harry Bassett takes up the cudgels on someone's behalf you can be sure he believes in their innocence. And usually he's right.'

'Usually,' Bob said morosely. 'By the law of averages he has to be wrong *once* in a lifetime. Do we leave it till tomorrow to tell him, or—?' He looked at Andy and Jim McPherson with a single glance, and screwed up his face.

Doc took the initiative. 'I'll go tell him.'

'Thought I'd give you the results of my findings as I usually do, Harry, first hand.'

'Good of you to come out, Jim.' Bassett hung up Doc's coat and scarf. 'Come and warm up by the fire.'

Drinks were poured, a fuss made of pup, then it was down to business. 'D'you want me to go into any detail—?'

'What you think will do me nicely, Jim.'

'I think Philip Read was hit with a bulk of wood,' Doc kicked off. 'Unpolished wood, could have been a log or branch of a tree. He and his assailant were standing. Read probably had his back to his assailant, began to turn round in response to a call or sound from behind him, and the assailant whacked him across face and head. A two-handed job, a baseball bat blow. Whoever did it either meant to kill—or else didn't give a damn whether they killed him or not. It was a vicious, hard-hitting attack, a hell of a lot of power behind it.

'The patch of ground you drew to the team's attention? The tests will have to be re-done, everything double checked, but I did find human blood in the soil samples. Also, traces of sawdust and bark on Read's suit. Traces only. No leafmould, fungus, insect debris, which would have been present if he had been killed in the woods. No evidence to suggest Read had lain in great amounts of sawdust. No evidence suggesting that he had been brushed down—'

Doc broke off, looked at Bassett for comment.

Bassett obliged. 'You mean, where Read lay at some stage may have appeared to be free of sawdust.'

'Yes. We think Robby Meddlar's woodshed. Or a room in the house; the kitchen or scullery, the traces left on the floor by someone who walked them in. The theory is that Robby Meddlar hit Philip Read, dragged or carried him into the woodshed, and when it was dark took him and buried him in the woods.'

'Buried him kindly,' Bassett murmured.

'You agree?' Doc was taken aback.

'Can't argue with the theory that Robby buried Read, Jim. He buried all the dead creatures he found. Tell me, though—when d'you think he wrapped Read in a blanket? Or let me put it another way: the blanket in the grave didn't seem to be heavily bloodstained.'

'There wouldn't have been a great amount of blood,' Doc said. 'Most would have come from nose, eye, mouth. Skull fractures were depressed, bleeding internal. The external bleeding would have slowed, even stopped, I think, fairly rapidly.'

'Provided he lay undisturbed for a while. He didn't die instantaneously?'

'No. He didn't live long either.'

'But there was a short gap in time. He could have been struck and left lying in the yard.'

'He could.'

'The murder weapon tossed into a hedge or to the back of Robby's woodpiles.' Bassett waggled eyebrows at his doctor friend. 'I don't think Robby killed lthe social worker, Jim. I think he came down from the woods and found Read lying in the yard. He's not violent but he is a nutter, there's no disputing that. He doesn't behave as normal people do. He's been brought up to be gentle, kind to animals, even dead animals. Sight of blood wouldn't upset him—he's seen blood before, on birds and other wild creatures he finds now and then in the woods. He buries dead creatures.

He buried Read. He may not even have waited until dark.'

Doc stared. 'He just wrapped Read in a blanket and buried him?'

Bassett nodded slowly. 'I don't think he'd have done it in haste. Have you ever found a dead or dying bird? I have. I imagine he saw the body. He'd have looked at it for a while. Lifted a hand to see if there was life there. In the end he took Read into his woodshed, cleaned up the mess outside, went and dug the grave, fetched an old blanket to wrap him in—he'd have had a box for a rabbit or bird—'

'Nightmarish, Harry.'

'To us. Not to Robby.' Bassett pursed his lips. Smiled. 'It's all right, I'm trying to figure out how one human being could bury another and not be affected by it. Bury in those circumstances. There's an answer. *The* answer. Robby saw nothing untowards in what he did.

'Can you get to see him, Jim? I think we asked him the wrong questions. Will you ask him the right ones? Don't expect an answer immediately. Ask again, the next day if you like. His thought processes are slow, he needs reminders, so I'm told. Keep at him—patiently—you, someone he's already met and has been kind to him, not a stranger, Jim; and I think in due course he'll tell you what I've just told you: that he *found* the body.'

'I think I need another drink, Harry.' Glass refilled, 'What makes you so sure Robby didn't strike the blow?'

'For one thing, he *said* he didn't, and I'm not sure he knows how to lie. For another, he would have been out in the open—on the face of it an unprovoked attack. *Why?*'

'Perhaps his mother goaded him.'

'No,' Bassett said. 'She taught him gentleness.'

'What if his mother wasn't there? I saw her shotgun at the station. If Robby has seen her threaten people with it— to clout someone is merely to take his mother's stance a step further.'

Bassett shook his head. 'I would guess that she only wielded it when Robby was missing. A deterrent. She lives in a lonely spot. She's against violence.'

'Anti-violence? Far be it from me to argue—' Doc kept it light—'but she does own a shotgun.'

'And has a reputation for using it,' Bassett replied in like manner. 'I know. Something wrong, isn't there? I've been puzzling over it myself. I think I have the explanation, Jim.'

He told Doc about Robby's background, and about Daniel. 'Robby runs from him, Daniel says. Runs from *Daniel*. Maybe because his mother instructed him to. Daniel is a gipsy. A settled gipsy, but a gipsy for all that. Alice wants no gipsy anywhere near Robby . . . Now, what people come unannounced to country houses? Not double-glazing salesmen. In Oakleigh we get gipsies, tinkers, dealers in scrap metal and old furniture, old pictures. *They* might have originated the shotgun tale. I've had them come to me— not Daniel's people, others, who refuse to take no for an answer. What's in the hut? What's in the barn? Any old furniture in there? *No*. Can we have a look? *No*, I've told you . . . If they did the same to Alice—'

'She wouldn't appreciate it,' Doc said.

'Exactly. Probably shook them up a bit. Phew! Who's the madwoman? Chased us with a blooming shotgun!' Bassett grinned. 'Could have happened years ago, Jim.'

Doc McPherson settled back in his chair. 'Go on. Tell me more.'

'I have a few ideas, Jim. Take Alice and Robby first, living their lives apart from the village for a quarter of a century; little contact with neighbours; no tradespeople calling until recently; no interference. The message was: Keep Out. In the main they were overlooked, there but rarely seen; seldom thought about.

'Peter Meddlar, Alice's husband, had been convicted of manslaughter. Who in the village knew? One person only. A lady, now old, who kept the information to herself. Later

two more people found out. One lives in America and told
no one; the other, again, kept it a secret. Then up pops Mrs
Mulholland, modern-thinking, good-hearted, agitating to
have Robby mixing with us so-called normal folk. And
suddenly the whole village knew about Robby's father. Odd,
Jim?

'I asked myself what prompted it. Had talk of bringing
Robby into the community spurred someone into placing
obstacles in the path? Robby on a short leash acceptable,
Robby on the loose, never! Or was it a kind of revenge?
Revenge by the family of the man Meddlar senior killed is
out. I'm waiting to hear if there is someone in Alice's past
with a motive for getting back at her in some way. But the
more I think of it the less sense it makes.'

'You mean someone killing Read for the express purpose
of Alice or Robby being blamed?'

'That was the route my mind was taking, Jim. It no
longer makes the sense it did. An old lady and her simpleton
son? There are any number of ways to hurt them—you
wouldn't have to kill an innocent man.'

'So . . . ?' Doc said.

'So I tracked down the old lady who started the rumour
about Robby's dad. She's senile, evil-tongued now; if people
took her seriously I would be forced to describe her as
malicious; but from what I've heard the majority of folk
don't. She blew the gaffe on Alice but no malice was intended. Unfortunately, however, her chatter led to Mrs
Mulholland bringing Philip Read into the picture. And *there*
I think we have it, Jim.

'I have a distinct feeling that Philip Read was not a victim
by chance, if you understand me. I have an idea he was
killed *because of who he was*.'

Here Bassett stopped and gazed steadily at Doc. Some of
the Doc's lost colour had returned to his cheeks. Could have
been the fire, could have been the whisky; it could have
been that Bassett hadn't disappointed him. Two elderly

men of like mind, one as keen to study a corpse for answers as the other was to study people, probe, worry his bone until he got at the truth: if one had begun to lose his grip, how soon the other?

'Because of who he was. You mean because he was a social worker?' Doc said.

Bassett nodded. 'I think it's possible. I've toyed with Alice Meddlar having recognized him as a figure from her past. No go. Philip Read wasn't old enough to have been a social worker when Robby was little. Alice Meddlar didn't recognize him. But what if someone else did? A newcomer with a Past.'

'Who?' Doc asked without thinking.

'That,' Bassett replied, 'is what we have to find out.'

CHAPTER 14

'Murder weapon.' Bob Greenaway slid a photograph across his desk to Bassett. It showed a long log bloodstained at one end.

Found where? In Robby's woodshed?

No. In undergrowth at the top of the track.

'On Meddlar property,' Bob said grimly. 'But not chucked there by either of the Meddlars.'

Bassett's eyebrows shot up. 'Fingerprints?'

Bob scowled. 'Don't get too excited. No, not a thing. But for one of the Meddlars to chuck that when they could have burnt it makes as much sense as burying Read in the woods and then marking the spot with a ruddy great bunch of flowers. OK, so maybe they don't make sense. Dippy, the pair of them. But to leave *that* lying around is plain stupid.'

Andy Miller: 'We think Read's attacker threw it down purposely to be found. Even if we didn't come up with the body on a routine search when Read was reported missing, we'd be sure to find the weapon.'

'I'm glad I came,' Bassett said comfortably. 'I very nearly didn't. Nearly went to gather more information first.' To have a chat with Mrs Brown, in fact; until it occurred to him that a mother of four would bless him for calling at nine o'clock in a morning.

Bob Greenaway received the photograph back. 'Doc told us the gist of your conversation last night. He mentioned that you were waiting for information concerning Mrs Meddlar's family.'

'Yes.' Bassett had that now. 'We can forget O'Connor, forget Mrs Meddlar's relations. Concentrate on Philip Read himself,' he suggested.

'This revenge idea,' said Andy. 'Revenge on Philip Read? For some job he muffed as a social worker? Bad judgement somewhere? Taking it upon himself to play God and getting it wrong? A mistake he made in the past?'

Bob Greenaway frowned. 'Someone with reason to hate him anyway.'

'Needn't be hate. Or revenge,' Bassett said. 'That was only my first thought. Could have been fear. Someone who was under the care of social services or under investigation, and now has a new life and a good position to maintain.'

'Recognized Read and was afraid he might give them away.' Andy speaking.

'Something like that, Andy.'

'He wouldn't have.' Andy again. 'More than his job was worth. But they mightn't have realized that.'

'What kind of person are we looking for?' Bob Greenaway's question. 'Ex-criminal? Drug addict? Baby-batterer? Shoplifter? Wife-beater?'

'Any of those,' Bassett said; although Bob had only been thinking aloud. 'Even someone from a bad home who suffers from false pride. Provided Mrs Read is in the clear. How'd you fare at Cheltenham?'

'Yep. I'd best bring you up to date.' Bob turned to his sergeant. 'Pull up a chair, Andy, you make the place untidy. And can't you do anything about that?' That was the cowlick Andy's hair had sprouted overnight. 'Tie a ribbon on it or something?'

Andy attempted to flatten the offending hair with both hands. Bassett grinned.

'What have we got?' Bob Greenaway said, straightening his face. 'We've got Read coming to Glevebourne last Saturday to buy a doll for his wife—she says. We know he bought the doll, we know he meant to drop in on the Meddlars. Mrs Meddlar says he didn't. She is OK, by the way. A minor attack, she should be able to go home in a week or ten days. Repeat, Mrs Meddlar says Read did not

visit her. Yet he got himself hit on the head in her yard.
And somebody stole the doll.'

He flicked Bassett a glance. 'I was curious to know
why Mrs Read and her husband took leave separately last
weekend, if you remember. No mystery, apparently. They
had arranged to have leave together several weeks previously, Mrs Read's course came up, the dates just happened to coincide. He decided not to cancel his but to use
the time catching up on DIY jobs at home. According to
his wife. Likewise, we only have her word for it that the doll
was bought for her—'

Bassett asked, 'Any reason not to believe her?'

'None.' Bob was merely pointing out the facts, he said.
'I wasn't satisfied with the reason she gave for leaving
Cheltenham on Friday when the course didn't begin until
Monday,' he continued. 'She said she had wanted to go to
a few retirement homes incognito. I told you she proposed
to open a home? Well, the plan was to pretend she was
shopping for a suitable place for an elderly relative, give the
establishments the once-over and form impressions. Seems
she spoke the truth: the list of homes she claims to have
visited all check out.

'Business course checked out, too. All open and above
board. No hint of monkey business at her hotel. No whiff
of shenanigans at home in Cheltenham or in the office—his
or hers. In short, they appeared to be happily married. No
motive therefore for Mrs Read to have wanted to get rid of
her husband.'

And 'happily married' automatically disposed of any
notion that Philip Read had a lady-friend tucked away near
Bletch Heath.

'I think—I should say I had a think about—what's her
name, the friend of Mrs Read's,' Bob said, rummaging
through papers on his desk. 'Here it is. Olivia Mulholland.
Seems she's in Scotland while her attractive sister, Mrs
Gray, stayed at home alone. Was there anything there? An

affair between Read and Mrs Gray? But one, we've just said Read was happily married; two, the Mulholland woman didn't leave for Scotland until Monday. Also, Mrs Read is adamant that last Saturday was the first time Mr had been to Bletch Heath. Proof is in a road atlas he bought himself. He left it behind, but he'd obviously studied the route—small tea or coffee stain on the appropriate page.'

From who was in the clear to who might not be.

'We're going to have another talk to the chap who reported the Datsun—the finder of the body often being the perpetrator of the crime. Granted, Collier found the *car*, but if it wasn't locked when found it could alter the picture considerably. Know much about him?'

'Ken Collier? Not a great deal,' Bassett said.

'Married. No children. Hippy type.' Bob Read from his notes. 'Not a local man. Our PC Taylor spoke to his wife routinely, she said her husband had mentioned the Datsun twice before he reported it to us. Anything to add?'

'You know as much as I do, Bob.'

'Cap in hand and tongue-tied here at the station. Could be he's recollected something else by now; never know your luck. In the meantime, no children means no little girl, means no known reason to have pinched the doll. Or the briefcase. Seems certain Read had the briefcase with him on Saturday. No trace of it at home. And that's about it.'

'You checked on the contents of the briefcase?' Bassett asked.

They had. Philip Read's office couldn't help.

'No files missing? Case notes?' Bob shook his head. 'Nothing photocopied on Friday, papers he wasn't allowed to remove from the office?' Answer: No. All had been checked. Weekend leave meant weekend leave: Philip Read wasn't even expecting to receive emergency calls.

'Yet the briefcase was stolen,' Andy observed.

'Not for its true contents,' Bassett suggested. 'Perhaps for what the thief *feared* it might contain.'

CHAPTER 17

'It certainly looks like the doll I sold to Mr Read. I had two dressed in maroon but only one wore spectacles.'

Bob Greenaway had brought the shopkeeper with him. He was grey-haired, genial; and outraged by what had befallen his customer. 'I can hardly believe it. Such a nice man. Friendly, telling me the doll was for his wife, a surprise she knew all about. We had some laughs over it, their womanly wiles.'

'My wife used to leave catalogues and magazines all over the house at Birthday and Christmas times,' Bassett put in, his face a hotch-potch of sentimental creases. 'Huge crosses everywhere. Could hardly find anywhere to sit in peace.'

Bob Greenaway fed him a look.

The shopkeeper continued unabashed. 'Trouble was, he couldn't remember which of the two she had set her heart on. She'd told him about the spectacles but she had also spoken about the pearl beads on the other doll. Tell her to come into the shop next time, I advised him, whisper her preference in my ear.' He spread a smile around, lapsed into silence as he studied the boxed doll from different angles.

'Yes, that's the doll,' he said decisively. 'He bought that one. Same box. The Sellotape strip holding the lid in place is different; otherwise it has to be the same doll. They're made by a small firm aiming at the exclusive. Be a remarkable coincidence if there were two identical in this area.'

'How did he make up his mind?' Bassett inquired. 'Did he ring someone up—?'

'No.' The shopkeeper gave Bassett a frank look. 'I offered him the use of the telephone, thinking his wife might have

He motioned towards the files in front of Bob Greenaway. 'This morning I was planning to call on a mother of four children. Last night I met an expectant mother. Everywhere I look I am reminded of children. Children. What do you have on Philip Read's work background?'

'The doll,' Bob muttered under his breath. He selected a file. 'He once worked on child abuse.'

They were back with Bassett's theory.

'Once worked,' Bassett murmured. 'Why not now?'

Bob scanned the notes in front of him. 'He spent something over two years in that field. Successfully. Excellent at the job. But got emotionally involved. Suffered a near nervous breakdown, tendered his resignation, which was refused. Given extended sick leave, then promoted to his present position in Cheltenham. Been in Cheltenham for three years.'

'Adding up to five years between the time his abuse work began and the present.' Andy sounded doubtful. 'Is that long enough for a kid to receive counselling, grow up, and embark on a new life?'

Ample time. Depending on the abused child's age.

'Spotty lads can turn into men, and gawky schoolgirls into charming young ladies overnight,' Bassett pointed out. 'How long did it take you, Andy, to grow hairs on your chest? Our killer doesn't have to have been a *victim* though, he or she could have been the abuser. The stigma would be as great, possibly worse. Nor does it have to have been sexual abuse; could have been neglect, cruelty, general ill-treatment—or sheer inadequacy.'

Bob Greenaway looked up from scribbling. 'What we want are details of Read's cases during the relevant period.'

'I'll give you some names,' Bassett said. 'Might lighten the load if you spot one of them.'

This done, Bob began reading them out. 'Brown. Gray. Mulholland. Collier . . . Mm, got to include him, I suppose. Herbert. Arthur. Who on earth are they? Be honest,

Harry—it could be anybody in Bletch Heath. You know
something else? It's not going to be easy gaining access to
this lot.'

'You'll manage it,' Bassett said. The flatterer.

From possible motive to opportunity. And a snag. According to Mrs Read nobody *knew* Philip was going to Glevebourne or Bletch Heath on Saturday. He could as easily
have chosen to go on the Monday or Tuesday of his leave.

'We've traced his movements from the shop where he
bought the doll to Bletch Heath war memorial,' Bob said.
'He was seen heading towards Cooper's Lane at around ten
o'clock. On paper that was the last anyone saw of him. There's
a telephone kiosk near the war memorial but he didn't stop
to make a phone call; and there are no houses between the war
memorial and Cooper's Lane. To all intents and purposes he
drove directly to the lay-by: end of story.'

'Sightings of the Datsun,' Bassett said.

Bob reached for a clipboard. 'Nothing useful.'

Bassett perused the list. 'You're collecting all sightings,
not only those on Saturday?'

'All,' was the reply. 'If Read *has* been in this area before,
unbeknowns to his wife, we want to know about it. Why?'

'Just a-wondering,' Bassett said, aping some of his village
friends. A-wondering why Ken Collier's wife hadn't told
PC Taylor that she had seen—thought she saw—the Datsun
outside Mrs Gray's house last week.

He let it go.

The telephone rang. Andy Miller took it; hand over the
mouthpiece, told them, 'Chap downstairs saw the Datsun
on Saturday—'

'Took him long enough to get here,' Bob growled. 'Go
see what he's got, Andy.'

'Calor Gas delivery man,' Andy told them when he returned. 'Says that at about ten a.m., give or take, he was in
Cooper's Lane driving towards the junction with the main
country road. A blue Ford Fiesta was coming *from* the

junction; it pulled into the lay-by to let him by. Pretty woman driving, baby in the back. When he reached the junction a car he believes was the Datsun was stationary some yards up on the left. He turned right, so didn't get a look at the driver or what the driver was doing, although he's pretty sure it was a man.

'Point is—' he patted the cowlick absently—'if *he* saw the Datsun the driver of the Fiesta must've seen it; but no owner of a Fiesta has come forward. The Calor man remembers a B and two 2s in the registration number . . . Sounds as if it might be young Mrs McDonald's.'

Only he, Andy, saw disappointment slide into the caring lines on Bassett's face. He looked away, at Bob, who was consulting a file.

A moment, and Bob was saying, 'On record she was in Glevebourne and elsewhere on Saturday. With other people, a Mrs Brown for one.' He looked at Bassett. 'She's sufficiently well-informed to be aware that we would check her alibi if necessary, so we may have a simple misunderstanding here. Our friend has taken his time getting here; it's possible he saw the Datsun last Saturday, the Fiesta pulling into the lay-by some other day, and his memory's playing him tricks.' A longer look at Bassett. 'Will you be seeing her today?'

Shortly afterwards Bassett was heading for Mayberry's supermarket with his Friday—weekend—shopping list. He derived no pleasure from his shopping; there was no touch of the connoisseur choosing the choicest fruit and vegetables, as was his custom; no begging to taste the special-offer Cheddar or the new bun loaf on promotion. He filled his trolley automatically and passed the time of day mechanically. He was familiar with Cooper's Lane now. For the bulk of its length the lane was narrow and winding, not unlike the lane in which he lived. The whole time the Calor Gas man was driving he would have been praying he wouldn't meet another vehicle, or if he did that it wouldn't be where he would be forced to reverse any distance. He would have been concentrating on his driving, and on the road. The Fiesta would have stuck in his mind.

Kathy had lied.

Back at the station Bob Greenaway added 'Mrs Kathy McDonald' to the list of suspects' names.

CHAPTER 15

Bassett decided to wait until after lunch to visit Kathy.
Lunch relating more to a meal than to time, he put his
shopping away, assisted by pup who always came in for a
treat on shopping days; cooked himself a dish of scrambled
eggs and shared the feast with pup. A glass of ale, a pipe
while he watched a programme about a wine-growing area
of France, an old haunt of his and Mary's, and he began
to shed the bone weariness that had threatened to overtake
him.

With renewed vitality came understanding: he now
understood why Kathy had lied about last Saturday. He
understood, that is, if Kathy had taken Alice shopping,
leaving Robby on his own.

He thought some more: about Mary; and his cleaning
lady, Sally. What would Sally have made of Alice? Mary
would probably have liked her.

Sally was on holiday, enjoying a well-earned rest. Meaning he had to do his own tidying up. He frequently did
anyway, never had taken kindly to someone else cleaning
up after him, but Sally added the extra touches, Mary's:
the polish, the flowers. It was Sally who on Tuesdays and
Fridays kept his home gleaming and sweet-smelling. Sally
without trying could restore flagging good humour simply
by coming out with some colourful observation on life . . .
Had she not been on holiday she would be here now, letting
slip a few titbits about the inhabitants of Bletch Heath,
courtesy of son John. Not that Sally gossiped. 'Ooh! not
me, Mr B. Ooh no! I'm no gossip, wouldn't do, me going
into so many houses, would it?' Bassett chuckled to himself.

Hey-ho, Sally wasn't available. He had never met her

son, perhaps he ought to. Time now, though, to go and speak to Kathy.

Kathy wasn't at home. He went on to Mrs Brown's. He had more questions to ask her today than he'd had last night.

He hesitated before pressing the bellpush and looked around. Large detached house, short wide drive, low front hedge. The Blossoms in full view from here and from the grassy garden at the side, where blankets were blowing gently on a line.

He pressed with a thumb. Hadn't long to wait.

'Mrs Brown?' Removing his hat.

She was about thirty, merrily untidy, quick with a smile. 'You're Mr Bassett!' The hat, the bearing, and pup sticky-beaking from the Citroën identified him; thus proving a point—that little went unremarked in a close-knit community.

'I've heard of you. Come in, do. You could have brought your dog, we're doggy people. And cats, mice, hamsters, rabbits, you name it—'

There were doors on either side of a spacious hall. Pam Brown indicated the furthest, ajar, a delicious smell of baking emanating. But muffled sounds were coming from a room on their left. 'Children?'

Finger to her lips, Pam beckoned, opened the door a crack. A blast of noise hit them: grunts and groans, squeals, giggles, and happy-dog barks. Then he was gazing upon a heap of arms and legs—seemingly hordes of children in a tangle on the playroom floor—with, sticking up in the middle, a great hairy tail wagging like mad.

'Meet my lot,' Pam Brown whispered.

Walls have ears. In a flash arms, legs and tail disentangled and materialized into five faces, four of them flushed and wearing wide-eyed startled smiles, the fifth, the hairy one, panting, all teeth and tongue.

'Hello,' Bassett said.

'Stay!' said their mother, command serving dog and children both.

'All yours?' Bassett inquired as the door shut them in.

'All mine!' was the radiant reply. 'Our doctor's fault. You're made for motherhood, Pam, he said; have a family quickly, get it over and done with. My husband played his part, of course. Tim and Andrew should be at school, but there's measles about and Tim was watery-eyed this morning, and Andrew was convinced he could feel spots developing. Did they look poorly to you?'

Bassett gave the answer expected of him. 'Fit as ticks, all of them!'

'I think so, too.' They went into a room next to the kitchen, a sort of hobbies room, whose french windows opened on to a barbecue and play area. 'I foresee a miraculous return to perfect health when it's time to collect Gran and Grandpa from the coach station.' An eyebrow arched pugnaciously: an idle threat to have it out with the children later.

'Sit down. What can I do for you?'

'Small query, Mrs Brown. You live almost opposite Mrs Gray and Mrs Mulholland. Did you not see a Datsun there last week?'

Her mouth fell for a second. 'I guessed it was that.' Confession time. 'I did see it, yes.'

'And omitted to tell the police.' A very mild reprimand.

And an equally mild plea for forgiveness. 'They were asking about a Mr Read. When I saw the car a woman got out of it.'

'You saw her.'

'A glimpse. As she went into the house. Truly I only saw her then because of Megan. Also I only saw a yellow car, I couldn't have sworn it was a Datsun.'

'Megan. The woman who was here last night?'

'Megan Collier, yes. She babysits for us.'

'Is she Ken Collier's wife?' Bassett said curiously.

'Yes.'

'Ah!' He broadened his smile. 'I begin to see. She was here—when was it?'

'Last Tuesday, I think.'

'That's right. Mr Collier mentioned that his wife had seen—she said a health visitor—leaving the car and entering Mrs Mulholland's. She didn't say anything to the police either. Same reason as you, I dare say. I suppose it *was* Mrs Read you saw, not Mrs Gray?'

'It couldn't have been Mrs Gray. We were up in the bedroom, I was trying on a dress I'd altered, and Megan was at the window. I went to see what was holding her attention. I've got babies on the brain, she said; I thought that was a nurse looking for me. A midwife, she meant, going across the road when she should have been coming here. Megan would have been watching her from the time she got out of the car.'

'A *nurse*. Why was that? Was she in uniform?'

'No.' Pam Brown laughed. 'You have to know Megan. She really does have babies on the brain. She and Ken have been trying for a baby for fifteen years. They'd given up hope. Then—it happened. We insist it was because she spent so much time with my four—it's catching. I'll be honest, Megan's a romancer. The day she told me she was expecting I thought oh, hello, another fib; especially when she made me promise to keep it a secret; it's not as if you can keep it a secret for ever, is it? But—' She broke off. 'I'm talking too much. You can't possibly be interested.'

'Oh, but I am,' Bassett assured her, returning the smile. 'Please go on.'

'I was going to say that Megan was brought up in an orphanage. So was Ken. She forgets, though, talks of family, nieces and nephews, sometimes. Her family is imaginary, she conjured it up in the orphanage so that she wouldn't be lonely. She even has a framed photograph of a supposed niece and nephew on a wall. I'm telling you—' Pam wrinkled her nose. 'Well, don't rely on all she says being the truth.'

Bassett rounded his mouth to an O. 'Understood. Any f'r 'instances—?'

'No, but to be forewarned—'

Bassett nodded and smiled agreement. 'Did Megan baby-sit for you last Saturday?'

'No, we didn't see her all weekend. Mrs Boon died. The farmer's wife. Where Ken works.'

'Ah, yes. She looked after the old lady.'

'And helped arrange everything. She's good in that respect. A godsend to me. Loves my boys.'

'Does she want a boy herself?' Bassett said, keeping it conversational.

'If it *is* catching, a boy is what she'll have!' Pam said merrily. 'She might even have the four. Carry on like this and Bletch Heath will soon have its own football team. Kathy McDonald's Michael—'

'You know Kathy, do you?' Bassett's voice swelled.

Getting to know her, Pam Brown told him. 'I'm afraid I put my big foot in it when she first arrived. Her wedding ring is so ancient it could be her grandmother's; and turning up when she did, just her and the baby, at Christmas time, when families normally all get together . . . I felt sure she was a single parent, unmarried or whatever. It even crossed my mind that she might have stolen the baby, like that woman in the news some months ago. She's still something of a mystery, doesn't say much about herself.' She shot a grimace at Bassett. 'Still, she's forgiven me.' Perkily.

She glanced at the carriage clock on a sideboard. A polite dismissal? Bassett rose. 'You're busy . . .'

Pam rose too, but was in no hurry. 'I've a cake in the oven but it will be all right for a while yet.'

Bassett twitched an eyebrow. 'Tell me then, what was the real reason for not mentioning the Datsun?'

Clearly Pam had thought that subject was closed. She wasn't pleased that he'd brought it up again.

'Harmony,' she said at last. 'If the constable had said: "Mrs Gray claims the Datsun was outside her house on such and such a day"—I would happily have said yes, I saw it. He didn't, he only asked if the Datsun had been in the area. I preferred ignorance; if Olivia and Annette were in trouble, well, I have to live here.'

'You were being neighbourly in other words.'

A nod. 'Have I got them into trouble now?'

'Good grief, no! Mrs Gray did tell the police herself. What about Saturday? Did you see the Datsun last Saturday?'

'No, not at all.'

'You were here?'

'Here and across the road. I popped across with a knitting pattern for Annette, and stopped for a cup of coffee with her and Olivia.'

'What time was this?'

'Between nine and half past.'

'Did either of them go out afterwards?'

'They both did. Annette answered the phone while I was there. She was telling someone how to get to a certain shop. I think she might have met the person later. Olivia left first, though; she went up to the bathroom and came down looking bored, said she'd nothing to read, she was going to the library. She put on her raincoat and we left the house together. Annette left shortly afterwards.'

'They have their own cars, don't share?'

'Annette has a Volkswagen Golf, Olivia a Fiesta.'

'Blue?' As they made for the door.

'White.'

'Were they out long?'

'I saw Annette come back, she can only have been out for half an hour. Olivia was out all morning.'

'No yellow Datsun, however. It didn't turn up while they were out?'

'No. I was in and out of the house for most of the morning, I would have seen it. Honestly.'

Bassett deliberately misunderstood the questioning frown. 'I believe you,' he said heartily; so making her laugh again. 'I've enjoyed our chat.' He held the door for her. 'Hope I haven't held you up too long . . . Megan lives near the farm, doesn't she?'

'She does. She won't be there this morning. I think you'll find her at the village hall this afternoon . . . Will you be going to the hall? You wouldn't like to do me a favour—?'

A doll she had dressed for the Bring and Buy Sale.

'The trouble with having all boys is that I never get to make pretty things. I dress dolls for fêtes and things instead.' She fetched a parcel from under the stairs. 'I'm very grateful. With the boys at home—'

Chatterbox, Bassett thought, as he drove away. Good neighbour; but not averse to throwing a poisoned dart or two: Megan Collier was a fibber, Kathy not all she pretended to be, if Pam Brown was to be believed.

Or had he misread her? Perhaps so.

He drove only a short distance, braked, untied the tape on the parcel.

It was a baby doll, all pink and white, ribbons and rosebuds; and cherubic smile.

CHAPTER 16

Kathy still wasn't at home. Neither was the woman who looked after baby Michael on occasion. They had both gone to the Women's Institute Bring and Buy Sale in the village hall. 'Gone early,' the woman's husband informed Bassett. 'They're doing refreshments.'

The man was a whittler. He had come to the door with a stick of pine in one hand, a knife in the other, and so had aroused Bassett's interest. 'Pensioned me off early. Dicky heart. But I can't sit doing nothing. You know what they say: idle hands . . .'

Bassett spent a pleasant five minutes in the man's workroom admiring his 'works of art'. A tiny place with barely room for table and chair; and shavings on the floor, not sawdust.

When Bassett left the house a familiar figure was standing by the gate collapsing an umbrella. There had been a shower of rain but already the sun was bursting through once more.

'The sun shines on the righteous!' Reverend Willy Brewerton exclaimed, meaning on Bassett.

'Ha! I thought the righteous shone for themselves!' Bassett replied, also meaning him.

'Saw your car,' Reverend Willy said as the two shook hands. His own treasured Morris Minor stood in the shelter of a tree some yards away.

'Can't escape for five minutes!' Bassett complained. 'You aren't following me by any chance? This is Bletch Heath, you know. Your church, Oakleigh, is thataway.'

He was standing in for his Bletch Heath counterpart, Willy explained, enjoying the banter. 'Hospital, hernia. He serves three parishes so I'm quite busy.'

'You can fit them in? Good grief! Does our Tod know?

He'll pull your leg unmercifully, William. He's forever saying you've so little to do at Oakleigh you might as well confess you're retired like the rest of us!'

'Then we won't tell him.' Willy lowered pale eyebrows, altered his voice. 'Is there any news?'

'About the murder?'

'Yes. Shocking business. Although one cannot help but feel pity for poor unfortunate Robby Meddlar.'

'Shame on you, Willy!'

'For heeding gossip and rumour?' The other's jaw dropped. 'I know,' he said with humility. His eyes fastened on to Bassett's with some discernment. 'You are working on it, naturally. If there's anything I can do . . .'

'Matter of fact there is.' A begging arm landed on Reverend Willy's shoulder. 'Women's Institute do on at the village hall. I'm duty bound to attend—'

'So am I.'

'Good! May I come with you? Men weren't made to attend these functions. Insufficient hands. You need one for your slice of cake, another for your cup and saucer. How do you then eat and drink and manage to talk all at the same time? Women have mastered the art, I alas never will.'

William giggled.

'Also,' Bassett confided woefully, 'they terrify me; the Big Noises, the Boss ladies. Remind me of the Mafia. I can see the hall now, packed to capacity with women. A hush descends as if on a signal. All eyes turn to the door, and there they are, making an entrance. The Godmother— wearing a Black Forest gâteau on her head—flanked on the left by a sixteen-stone Enforcer, on the right by a thin bespectacled Mouthpiece—'

'The Consigliere,' put in Willy.

'The Consigliere—' Bassett stopped short. 'Good grief! Where did you learn such things, Willy?'

Reverend Willy giggled again. 'Have you ever been to a WI do?'

'Not for years,' Bassett admitted.

'You might be pleasantly surprised.'

It was so. The President of the local WI turned out to be a personable one-time gym teacher; and—'Her Henchpersons,' Willy whispered wickedly, pointing them out, were a young farmer's wife and a professional cook.

It was they themselves, Bassett and the Reverend, who made the Entrance and caused a hush to descend. Briefly. The President detached herself from a band of helpers and the buzz of activity picked up again.

She greeted them warmly. 'Reverend Brewerton! How nice to see you!' And, 'Oh, how wonderful!' to Bassett after introductions. 'You're the superannuated policeman I've been hearing about!'

'Chief superannuated, if you please.'

He had sized her up correctly: she laughed, delighted. He lost his nervousness. 'My ladies would adore to hear about some of your experiences. Would you give a talk one day? They'd be thrilled.' And to William, waving a hand towards laden tables and hives of industry, 'What do you think?'

'Splendid.'

'We've some delicious marmalade and chutneys. Excellent chutneys if you are a pickle man—'

This also to Bassett, who belatedly held out the parcel he was carrying. 'From Mrs Brown, with apologies for not bringing it herself. Her boys may be sickening for measles.'

'Oh, poor Mrs Brown. How kind of her! Of you too, for bringing it.' She was wanted. 'Can you amuse yourselves for a while? Sale opens officially at two-thirty, gives mothers an hour before they have to trot next door to collect their children from school.'

They watched her go.

'Something else you might do for me, Willy,' Bassett said presently. 'Two young women. The one with pretty black hair, see her, with the baby? And the blonde woman with pinched features—there, armful of woollens. Get your best

Sunday smile out—ask them, separately of course, if you
haven't seen them before, when they were youngsters or
something: were they at your Sunday School.'

'What am I to listen out for?'

'Names before they were married, if you can. Otherwise
make sure I can see their faces, that's all. I want to see their
reactions.'

'Very well. I'm off to mingle.'

William mingled. Kathy espied Bassett, was about to
come to him, but was drawn back into the kitchen. Behind
him someone was exclaiming over lavender bags and pot-
pourri. Near the tombola two women were in a huddle
tittering over an item they had unpacked from a large
holdall. No one mentioned murder or mysterious goings-on
or Robby Meddlar . . . Willy had paused, hands behind his
back, to watch Mrs Collier drape a blouse on to a hanger;
he leaned across a table of jumpers and cardigans to speak
to her; she smiled shyly . . .

Ten seconds . . . ten more . . . Questions asked. And
answered. A seemingly light-hearted exchange.

'Maiden name, Thomas,' Willy told Bassett in passing.
Kathy was trotting out of the kitchen, Willy moved to
intercept her.

And a cry went up in the 'Something Special' corner.

A cry of joy. 'Isn't she a darling! Look, Freda, at this
gorgeous doll!'

Mrs Brown's, Bassett supposed. But several helpers were
converging on the corner, and their silencers were off, no
one spoke quietly. 'Who's the generous one? Have you seen
what they *cost*?—' 'That new shop in town, I was looking
at them the other day.—' 'Nobody will be able to afford
her. I think we ought to raffle her, be fairer.—' 'But who
brought the doll in?' someone asked extra loudly.

No one owned up.

'May I?' Bassett said. Room was made for him.

He stared down at a china doll in Victorian dress:

maroon velvet, lace, straw boater, and the daintiest pair of gold-rimmed spectacles; packed in a high-quality transparent box. 'Ladies, may I ask you not to touch it?' Many of them already had.

Murmurs of dissent. 'Oh . . .'

The President took charge. 'Mr Bassett is right. The doll may have got here by mistake. It's obviously new. Until we find out—'

'Let me have a last look.' A young fun-loving woman shouldered her way to the front. 'Look, Anne, isn't she sweet?' The two crooned, a third woman, pale-faced and silent, smiled indulgently on. Willy looked mystified. Bassett, wiping his nose, drew the WI President aside.

'Bring and Buy,' he sniffed. 'People bring an item, buy an item. Am I right?'

'That is the general idea, yes. Although we have loads in store usually, jumble-sale stuff and so on.'

'Held in store.' Bassett's glances took in black plastic refuse bags and cardboard boxes at various stages of being emptied. 'I think until we know more about the doll we should withdraw it.'

'You think the doll could be stolen property?' the lady whispered astutely.

'It is possible. No fuss though. No call to spoil the afternoon. Carry on as normal. I don't want your ladies to leave until I've spoken to them, however. Better still, as we don't want to put a damper on the afternoon, could someone make a list—'

'I'll get Anne to do it. She knows everybody . . . We have a small room, our glory hole. We could fix it up with a table and chair, and in the meantime I shall ask around and see what I can find out.'

'There does appear to be a mystery,' the President informed Bassett in the glory hole. 'Megan Collier was first in after lunch, about one o'clock. The doll was on a chair just inside the door, she says. But Clem, he's our handyman, who unlocked the door to let Megan in, had locked the door at midday, and he insists the doll wasn't there then.'

'Good news, Mrs McFaddien.'

'Is it?' She failed to see how.

'We have a start,' Bassett said, elated. 'I fully expected the doll to have appeared out of thin air, no one having seen it *ever*.'

'Oh,' she said with a little laugh, 'I hadn't thought of that. I'll ask Megan to come in, shall I?'

At 2.30 the Bring and Buy Sale was declared open.

By three o'clock Bassett had spoken to all the women with information to impart, and was talking to Inspector Bob Greenaway from the public telephone kiosk by the school next door. 'I'm at a Bring and Buy Sale, Bob. Bletch Heath village hall. A doll answering the description of the one Philip Read purchased has turned up here . . .'

He didn't return to the hall; he walked the grounds, mentally sifting through his notes.

Megan Collier said she saw the doll on the chair when she entered the hall at one o'clock.

Bassett: 'Tell me exactly what you did when you got here at one o'clock.'

Megan: 'Clem unlocked the door when he saw me coming.'

'You came by car?'

'Yes.'

'Anyone else arriving at the same time?'

'I didn't see anybody.'

'Did you actually see Clem unlock the door, or did you assume he unlocked it?'

She saw him, Megan said. Clem unlocked the door, waited for her, gave the door a push. There you are, love, he'd said. He hadn't gone in with her.

Bassett: 'You were alone when you went in and saw the boxed doll.'

Megan: 'I didn't notice it straight away. I started work on my table, then I noticed the box.'

'Were you still alone?'

'Yes. Kathy McDonald stuck her head inside the door and went off again. She was looking for Jill.'

'It was after Mrs McDonald looked in that you saw the box?'

'Yes,' Megan said. 'But Kathy couldn't have put it there. I'd have seen her.'

'Were you missing at any time?' he'd asked her.

'I did go to spend a penny.' Hesitation here.

'The room next to this.'

'Yes.'

'Think carefully. Did you take the doll to the sorting table before you went to spend a penny?'

'No, it must have been afterwards. I'd just put it on the table when Helga and Betty arrived.'

'So the doll may *not* have been on the chair at one o'clock. It may have been put there while you were spending a penny. You assumed when you spotted it, as you had been the only one there, that the doll had been on the chair all along.'

'Yes, I suppose I did.'

Not a very bright lady; one who evoked sympathy for no particular reason that he could think of.

He had smiled at her then. 'Bring and Buy. May I inquire what you brought, Mrs Collier?'

'A cake. We haven't got much to give away. And some paperbacks and magazines. Coll brought those for me this morning.' Coll was Colin Bryan, the man who worked with her husband at Boon's Farm.

'Can I ask you something?' she had said when he thanked her and told her she could go for now. 'The man who was found in the woods. Is this anything to do with him?'

'Can you help in any way, Mrs Collier?'

'No.' Her smile was sad. 'It's such a pretty doll.'

He had seen Clem next: gardener at Bletch House, honorary handyman here by tradition. Clem cut the grass, attended to the water heater and generally got everything ready for the ladies.

He had definitely locked up at midday, Clem said. He'd arrived back more or less at the same time as Mrs Collier, was getting out of his van as she had pulled in. He'd called to her that he would unlock the door, and had done just that.

No, he hadn't entered the hall himself. Had he looked in? At midday, yes: to make sure the place was empty. Not when he *un*locked the door; no cause to.

Clem hadn't seen the doll before. He confirmed that Megan had only been carrying a small handbag and a biscuit tin. 'Cake in it the lass had made for the teas.'

He also corroborated her order of first-comers. After Megan, Kathy McDonald. Then Helga and her mate, Betty. Jill Morris. Mrs Gray.

Kathy had fled the car park to go to the hall, was back seconds later asking him if he would keep an eye on her little 'un, Clem said. He had helped her get the folding pram out of her car, and she had gone to fetch Dot Gurney and Cissie Beardmore.

Mrs Gray had dropped off a box of plants. Clem had taken them to the hall for her.

None of the first arrivals had been carrying anything large enough to contain the boxed doll in Clem's opinion.

Helga and Betty had been the next questioned. Megan said that she had put the doll on the sorting table bare moments before Helga and Betty turned up. The two friends endorsed this by saying that Megan had been leaving the table when they arrived. But Helga put her own interpretation on Megan's leaving empty-handed: she thought Megan looked guilty—'as if she had been going to steal something'. Neither of them had seen the doll, they hadn't needed to go to the sorting table.

Odd one, Helga. Assumed pleasantness but was quite
bitchy underneath.

The two sorters, one of them the playful Anne, explained
why the doll had remained on their table for nearly an hour
before being allocated. They had thought the doll and the
woolly garment on top had been put to one side, reserved
so to speak. They hadn't looked at it properly, too many
bags and boxes requiring their attention. It had been the
lady in charge of 'Something Special' who eventually nosed
it out. She had taken the doll to her table, and only on closer
inspection realized what she had.

Nothing suspicious there.

Kathy had been surprised when he fetched her. 'Me, Mr
Bassett? I haven't even seen the doll, it was whisked off
before I got a peep.'

'Look now, Kathy. Don't touch!' She fell in love with it.
Had she seen it before?

She had seen one like it, she said. 'In that new shop in
Glevebourne. Is that where this is from? Mrs McFaddien
says it probably got here by mistake.'

'It was found on the chair by the door at one o'clock. Did
you see it when you looked in?'

'Can't remember seeing anything. I didn't look . . .' She
cast her mind back, shook her head. 'It *might* have been on
the chair, there were things littered all over the show.'

What had the head round the door been all about? he
had asked her.

She had been looking for Jill Morris, she said; she wanted
Jill to mind the baby for a while. Pam Brown had been
going to ferry ladies who were without transport, couldn't
at the last minute, her boys had spots, she had agreed to
do it instead.   .

Yes, in reply to his next question, neighbours would
normally travel in the same car, but Jill had to collect her
son from Glevebourne Comprehensive later so they chose
to be independent of each other. And yes, she had noticed

Jill's car wasn't in the car park, but you can't always believe what you see, can you? Mr Morris might have wanted the car for an hour and dropped Jill off.

All of which made perfect sense.

What had Megan been doing when Kathy stuck her head round the door? She had been standing by her own table, Kathy said. Which, again, fitted in with Mrs Collier's story.

Bassett had now been all round the outside of the building, taking stock. The fire door was, against the rules, locked and bolted. There was no back door. No access via windows. Spare keys had been accounted for by Mrs McFaddien. The only opportunity anyone had of sneaking the doll in seemed to be when Megan Collier was in the lavatory; a sneak on foot, able to avoid Clem's watchful eye and other arrivals.

Or else *the doll had never been on the chair by the door.*

a friend who would know. Apparently not. Her passion for dolls was to remain forever a secret, it was bad enough him teasing her. Can't think why she felt like that,' he said, vaguely bewildered. 'They are as much collectors' pieces as toys.'

After the shopkeeper had gone Bassett supplied Bob and Andy with a résumé of his investigations so far.

'The media know nothing about a doll or briefcase,' Bob said. 'Wonder what made our killer decide to get rid of it.'

'Could have made a gift of it to someone, guv?' Andy said. 'And the someone guessed where he got it.'

'And hadn't the heart to smash it, burn it, or toss it on a rubbish dump. Smuggles it in here, get rid of it that way. Let it go to a new home. Only it backfired.' Bob turned to Bassett. 'The woman who worked out that it might be stolen property—'

'President of the WI, Bob. Unlikely suspect.'

'Pity.' Bob gestured to Andy. 'We'd better get cracking. Compare notes with you later, Harry. Unless you would like to sit in.'

'No. I'll potter. And I've still to have that chat with Kathy McDonald about last Saturday.'

'We'll see her first then, preliminaries only. We can get back to her later.'

Bassett hunted Kathy out. 'Inspector Greenaway will be wanting you shortly. When he's through I'd like you and me to take a little trip.'

From Kathy to Reverend Brewerton. 'We are browsing, Willy,' Bassett said, steering him in the direction of a particular table.

'Are we? And are we enjoying it?'

At the table Bassett picked up a jar with a fancy muslin top, labelled Pot-Pourri; he sniffed, replaced the jar, idled on a pace, and picked up a lavender bag. 'Refreshing,' he said to the woman serving. 'My mother used to have lavender sticks hanging in her wardrobes.'

He picked up a larger bag. 'That's pot-pourri as well,' the woman advised. 'I prefer it myself. A more delicate perfume.'

'It is like this,' Bassett said agreeably, sniffing the bag. 'What do you think, William?' Not waiting for Willy's reply, he said to the woman, 'Is this the same as in the jar?'

'Yes. The jar is for standing in a room.'

'Ah, I see. Where does it come from?'

'Mrs Boon.'

'Old Mrs Boon, from the farm?'

'Yes.' The woman addressed William. 'Very kind of Mr Boon to send it as normal, wasn't it, Vicar.'

'Indeed.'

'Mrs Boon made her lavender bags and pot-pourri for us for more years than I care to remember.' Informatively now, a chaste smile appearing. 'Church fêtes and our sales have never been without them.'

'I'll have one of each,' Bassett said. 'The jar, a bag of pot-pourri, and a lavender bag. Would you wrap them for me, please.'

From the scent table to the President, to ask if he might see the container the pot-pourri had come in.

'Freezer bags,' she whispered helpfully. 'I should be able to fish them out.'

'Freezer bags? I expected something larger.'

'Oh. Oh yes. They were in a black dustbin bag. I put it in the cupboard in the glory hole while we were waiting for the Inspector. One of two bags. You can't mistake them. The other contains some of Mrs Boon's clothes. We didn't unpack them; rather too close to—well, the funeral was only two days ago. We'll bring them out next time.'

'We could drift in that direction,' Bassett said to Reverend Willy.

When it was convenient, a word to Bob Greenaway. 'In the cupboard, Bob. Two black plastic bags. May be evidence. These too. Pot-pourri and lavender.'

Then it was into the grounds for a further chat.

'You officiated at the funeral, Willy.'

'Yes, I did.'

'And knowing you, you wouldn't have done it blind. What can you tell me about the men who work at the farm? One named Coll—Colin. He told me the Boons took him in. By which I took it to mean they gave him a home.'

Willy nodded. 'Colin's mother died when he was little. He didn't get on with his stepmother. Left home when he was sixteen, finally ended up at the Boon house asking for summer work. He was taken on and has been there ever since.'

'A sort of adopted son?'

'Yes, I believe so, eventually. Mrs Boon's doing. She had been an orphan herself and so was determined that her husband employed people who needed a chance in life. Before Colin there had been a man like him, homeless and friendless; but he left, moved to a smallholding. I met him at the funeral. Method in their benevolence, he said; they paid low wages, a good home compensated. Small farm, never employed more than one full-timer until a year or two ago, when Mr Boon began feeling his age.

'That was when they took on Mr Collier. He couldn't praise Mrs Boon highly enough. He and his wife were destitute after his business failed. When he applied for the labouring job he never imagined he would get it. Over the moon when he did.

'I fancy that when he used the word business Mr Collier was being coy. He was actually an unsuccessful pop singer, so Colin told me. Finally he grew up, and has settled down to what we who live in the country are pleased to call the good life.'

'Sincere?' Bassett said.

'I'm sure of it,' Reverend Willy replied firmly. 'If you had seen his face when he was telling me. Life has never been so good to him as now. That much he told me himself. It

was the pop group he fought shy of. Perhaps he thinks we
vicars are all squares!'

'The other man, Colin, never married.'

'His eye, I fancy. Considers himself unattractive. It's
hardly noticeable. No disfigurement. Not to me, at any rate.
And not to the right woman, I'm sure, if she should happen
along.'

'How did he get his eye, Willy?'

Ill-treatment?

'Accident with an air rifle, I believe, when he was a
youngster . . . Ah!' Willy's voice went high. 'I see the young
lady with the black hair.' Kathy had come into view round
a corner of the building. 'I never did ask her that question.'

'Her name is Kathy McDonald, and it doesn't matter
now,' Bassett said. 'I think she's after me.' He waved,
signalled five minutes, and as Kathy retreated said to Willy,
'You had already met Mrs Collier.'

'At Mrs Boon's, yes. I had never been in conversation
with her though, so my curiosity on your behalf would have
seemed perfectly normal. Was I of help?' Willy wanted to
know. 'If so, please tell me what is going on! Dolls—
pot-pourri—dustbin bags!'

'The doll's box smells of perfume, Willy; the same as the
pot-pourri.'

'You think the doll arrived with the pot-pourri.'

'I *did*. But Mrs Boon's perfumed goods are sold every
year. Half the village will have them in their wardrobes and
cubbyholes. So—' Bassett shrugged.

And touched Willy's sleeve. 'There's Clem. I need to
speak to him.'

Willy's cue to make himself scarce.

Clem was on his haunches on the grass watching a column
of ants. Bassett lowered himself alongside.

'Mind if we go over a few items, Clem? Blooming nuisance, I know, having to repeat yourself. Would you tell me
again what you did and saw from one o'clock on.'

Clem was happy to. Nothing changed in the telling.

'Mrs Gray dropped a parcel off,' Bassett said.

'A box of plants.' Clem had seen her struggling to lift the box out of her car, had gone and offered to carry it in for her. She hadn't gone with him. He had seen her drive off.

'Do many people do that? Drop bags and boxes off?'

'Some,' Clem said. Box of stuff outside the door when he arrived that morning: from the shop, that one, Des Arthur had brought it. And as he was about to lock up at midday Coll Bryan delivered two bags and a box. The box was Mrs Collier's. Clem knew, he said, because he carried it in for Coll and the bottom dropped out. 'Full of magazines and books.'

'Were there people here in the morning, Clem?'

One or two. Clem named them: names unfamiliar to Bassett. 'Kathy not here? Mrs Collier, Mrs Morris?'

'Not that I saw,' Clem said.

'And you were just on the verge of locking up when Coll Bryan arrived. He carried in the bags. You had the box. The bottom fell out. Coll helped you gather up the books?' Answer: yes. 'Which of you was last out?'

They left together, Clem said.

'You'd already looked round to make sure no one was locked in. And the doll definitely wasn't on the chair.'

Couldn't have been, said Clem. 'I put the box the magazines came in on the chair while we were picking the books and magazines up.'

Bassett sighed. 'Thank you, Clem.'

Kathy was waiting by his Citroën with the pram. 'Did Inspector Greenaway say anything to you about last Saturday morning, Kathy?'

She searched Bassett's face; a miserable five seconds, then twitched the corners of her mouth. 'I knew the Calor Gas man would split on me some time, I wanted a little breathing space.'

'You mean you wanted me to have breathing space.'
Bassett assisted her with the pram. 'Come on, young fellow
me lad! We're going to Alice's. You first, Kathy, I'll follow.'

CHAPTER 18

Bassett overtook Kathy's Fiesta as they drove up to the war memorial. He signalled her to stop, parked his own car at the edge of the green, joined her as passenger.

'Better this way. Now tell me about Saturday. What happened?'

'Nothing happened,' Kathy said. 'I was going to town, went to see if Alice wanted to come shopping. She didn't, but she had a lift to the post-box, the one by the memorial, this one; she said she would walk back. I went on to Glevebourne.'

'Spent the whole day there.'

'No. There was a Model Show on in the deer park. Model aeroplanes, helicopters; ships and yachts on the lake. I hadn't planned it but as I was driving home I saw the caravans and marquees and crowds of people in a field, and decided to stop; I was thinking of Robby, Mrs Mulholland did have a point, he could have gone out more. It was her domineering attitude I resented, and I've known perfectly normal people who were quite happy to be stay-at-homes ... Anyhow, an open-air show—I thought I might talk Alice into bringing Robby. I went to have a look and it was so entertaining—a mock Battle of Britain, aerobatics, comedy stunts—I stayed. Found out it was a two-day event anyway, so I could always bring them the next day, Sunday.'

'And on the way home you called in to invite them.'

'No, I went straight home. The baby was tired, he'd had an exciting day. Also I had only one nappy change with me.'

'You met people you know at the show?'

'Mr and Mrs Brown and their boys. I spent the afternoon with them, we all left together.'

'You went straight home. Did you see Alice or Robby on Saturday evening? No. You went on Sunday—'

'No, I had second thoughts. To spring an outing on Robby might not be a good idea. I decided to tell him and Alice about it and suggest that the next open-air event, in the summer, well, we might all go.'

'You said you dropped his mother off at the post-box.'

Kathy nodded. 'A letter. I offered to post it for her but she wanted to post it herself.'

'You saw the letter?'

'It was to Mottram's, the antique dealers. The one which brought the reply we found, probably.'

Posted *before* the Datsun's appearance; so forget fleeing money. However . . .

'Why wouldn't Alice let you post it for her?'

'Habit?' Kathy said. 'She wasn't accustomed ro people doing her favours. Also, she may have forgotten I knew why she wrote to Mottram's. I'm possibly the only person outside Mottram's who knows about her transactions, and I was sworn to secrecy. What people had no knowledge of they couldn't rob her of, she said. There had been burglary attempts in the past.'

'She seems to have been remarkably open with you, Kathy.'

'I wish she hadn't been, honestly I do,' Kathy said, with a rare attack of despondency. 'I don't want the responsibility. There was a reason for her confiding in me. She didn't believe my story—that Mike is overseas, and that I decided all in a rush to move out of our flat and into the cottage. She was convinced I was in the same boat as herself—alone with a child. How would I live? What would I do for money? She was lucky, she said; when her money ran out she had assets to fall back on. She was getting old, wouldn't live for ever. She would see that I was all right financially if . . . *if*. She never did complete the sentence, but over and over again she told me Robby was no trouble. I got the message: I would benefit in exchange for looking after Robby.'

'Which you can't do if you join your husband in—where was it? Dubai?'

'Qatar.'

'I'm an old man myself, Kathy. It is against my nature to be anything but polite to charming ladies. I fear I am now going to be rather *im*polite. Have you no family? You see, you are something of a mystery.'

'Because I turned up here when I did? Season of goodwill and all that? What on earth were my folks doing letting me take off into the blue? And the cottage wasn't even ready to live in? Oh, I've heard the gossip.' Kathy's eyes flashed angrily. 'I am not a child and I've never been tied to my mother's apron strings. I was brought up to be independent. I went to boarding-school when I was eight, and in my case it was perhaps the best thing that could have happened, because when my mother died two years later I didn't miss her as much as I might otherwise have done. I carried on as before, holidays with my dad or with my schoolfriends and their families.

'I considered myself lucky. I enjoyed my life. As for my dad, where is he? He's in the diplomatic service abroad. I was a disappointment to him: after my education, the money he'd spent on me, he expected me to marry, quote, "Well". I chose a penniless council house fella, Mike, who's going to make his own way in the world . . . Our flat *was* expensive, I *was* going to move out in the spring. But I overheard two of Mike's cousins talking. To the effect that I had no right to Forge Cottage, lucky old me! Spoilt rotten. If I fell off a multi-storey building I'd fall into a new dress. One of them had a friend who wanted the cottage, an artist or something. They were hatching a plot to install the artist on the quiet in the New Year—and hard luck, Kathy.

'That was why I nipped off when I did, I wanted to be in the cottage before Christmas, a fixture by the time the cousins turned up. And that was why I accepted Mrs Meddlar's invitation to spend Christmas with her and Robby rather than find a hotel. Being next door so to speak, I could pop to the cottage every day, make it look lived in even without electricity.'

She stopped, ran her hands down both cheeks. 'Sorry, I didn't mean to sound off at you. But people make me cross sometimes.'

'Would you like an ice-cream?' Bassett said. 'Shop back there.'

Kathy gave him a profile look, then burst into laughter. 'Honestly . . . !' Good humour restored.

They left the war memorial behind. Kathy slowed the Fiesta. 'It was about here . . .' where she saw what could have been the Datsun in front of her. 'It was crawling, as if the driver was looking for a place to park up. I didn't overtake, the turn-off was ahead.'

The turn-off to Cooper's Lane, the lay-by, and Alice Meddlar's house.

'He passed the turn-off—'

'But you did not,' Bassett said. 'Take the turn, then stop for a second. Good. Where was the Datsun?'

'Driving on.'

'Towards Boon's Farm?'

'Yes.'

'What else did you see?'

'A tractor. Way up. I could hear it.'

'Fine. Drive on. You pulled in to the lay-by to let the Calor man by—a minute, say. On then to Alice's. Don't go there, keep going till you can turn round and come back.'

Kathy drove, Bassett talked. 'At Alice's for how long? Five minutes, ten at most. Right. You leave Alice's. Anything in the lay-by on the return?'

'No.'

'On to the junction, where you stop, look to the left. Look now . . . Think back. What did you see?'

'Nothing. The road was empty.'

'No Datsun?'

'No Datsun.'

'The tractor?'

'Still there. I don't think it had moved.'

'No one on foot? No activity near the farm?'

'None that I could see.'

'You had Alice with you. Might she have blocked your view?'

Kathy shook her head. 'She was in the back with the baby.'

'Where was Robby when you collected Alice?'

'Where he is most mornings, I imagine, logging.'

'Suppose he wasn't, suppose he was in the house; and suppose the Datsun drove on, and round, and came down Cooper's Lane same as the Calor man. Suppose Mr Read went to the house, knocked on the door—'

'Robby wouldn't have answered it. He opens the door to nobody.'

'Yet when you learnt about the Datsun being found, driver missing, you thought he had. It occurred to you that the Datsun hadn't been looking for a place to park, he had been looking for an address, Alice's; and found it, while Alice was walking from the post-box and Robby was alone.'

'No, Mr Bassett. I knew that if I told the police that Robby had been alone, for what was probably as long as an hour, I might have started something. I didn't lie to you; you asked if I could prove where I was on Saturday, I said I could. You asked if I saw Robby on Saturday, I said I hadn't. Both true.'

'Then I must be careful how I put this next question. Do you know anything whatsoever about the death of Mr Read?'

'Absolutely nothing.'

They stared at each other in silence, the one anxious yet spirited, the other contemplative.

Bassett was the first to speak. 'Suppose when Alice got back from her walk she found Robby and Philip Read hitting it off well, Robby all excited—'

'She wouldn't have attacked the man,' Kathy said, aghast. 'People have the wrong picture of Alice. She wouldn't have done anything to ruin Robby's chances. I think she's worried about Robby's future, I think she realizes she's left it late; but she did once say she had a relation, of whom she now approved, who would take Robby in if necessary. The relation grows trees, deciduous trees for new woodland, hedge restoration and so on. Robby would be as happy there as anywhere.'

With Daniel. Daniel and his tree nurseries.

'She didn't do it,' Kathy said vehemently. 'She *wouldn't*. Nor would Robby. Why would either of them—'

Bassett held up a finger. 'I believe you.'

What? At last it sank in. 'I wish all policemen were like you,' Kathy said warmly. She leant over and plonked a kiss on his cheek.

'Ta.' Bassett received his mug of tea from Andy Miller and sipped gratefully. 'Mmm. This is going down well.' He, Bob and Andy had met up in Bob's office to compare notes.

One minor difference: Megan Collier had admitted she had been tempted to steal the doll. Her baby might be a girl, and her husband's wages would never run to buying a doll so pretty. Otherwise she stuck to her story.

'Don't know whether she was nervous or naturally dull and—' Bob sought for the right word.

'Unhappy?' Bassett finished for him.

Fingerprints. No use bothering until they knew they had a decent one to play with; but all those asked had agreed to cooperate, save for one. 'Who was that?' Bassett asked. Answer, with a grin, 'Mrs McFaddlen, the Boss lady.' She had said yes, provided she could witness the destruction of her prints when she had been eliminated from inquiries. Someone else, to Andy's amusement, had wanted to know if it meant they would end up as 'mug-shots'.

'Got your pen ready?' Bassett said. ''Nother name. Colin Bryan, works at the farm where the pot-pourri came from.'

Bob wrote. 'Is that the chap who delivered those bags to the village hall? What have you got on him?'

'Nothing, Bob. While you're at it jot down Thomas. That's Mrs Collier's maiden name. They've been married for fifteen years, so I've been told, but it won't hurt for you to have it.'

Bassett then recounted the gist of his talk with Kathy McDonald. 'Fits in with the Calor man's story. We know the social worker wasn't familiar with Bletch Heath. If he missed the turn-off, saw the tractor up ahead—' Could be he'd carried on to the farm to seek directions.

Bob addressed his sergeant. 'Feel fit, Andy?'

'Do I have any choice?' Andy said, rising.

CHAPTER 19

Bassett parked on the green as he had earlier when with Kathy, and got into the back of the police car.

'Mrs McDonald picked up the Datsun about here,' he said as they circled the war memorial. 'It passed the turn-off Locals and the postie know it's Cooper's Lane turn-off, a stranger wouldn't.'

'Hold your foot up,' Bob Greenaway grouched; 'we haven't sighted the turn-off yet.' Presently they did reach it. 'OK, let's see what he would have done next. He was stationary when the Calor man saw him—'

'He saw the Fiesta go into the lane, the Calor truck come out, thought: Ah! civilization up there!—backed up, and went for a look-see,' Andy said from the driver's seat.

'So where was he when Kathy left Alice's ten or fifteen minutes later?' Bassett said. 'He wasn't in the lay-by.'

'He missed the track, carried on till he got to the other end of Cooper's Lane, turned round and came back.' Andy again.

'In which case he would have been nose-pointed towards the junction,' Bassett said. 'He wasn't. He parked t'other way round in the lay-by . . . No, I think he stopped to gather his bearings, saw the tractor up ahead, went on to the farm. It's what I would've done. Tractor-driver—neighbour—neighbour should know where the Meddlars lived.'

They drove on to the farm. 'House on the right,' Bob said. 'Set well back. Could easily miss it, but if he was on the lookout—'

'That's the Collier house,' Bassett said.

Bob half turned in his seat. 'The Collier who reported the Datsun? . . . Drive on, MacDuff!'—to Andy. 'If he'd gone there we'd have heard about it.'

Bassett was silent.

The farm was sleepy, having a tea-break. Andy sauntered off to put his head inside sheds and barns; the farmer's wife having died a week ago, this was a house of bereavement: two clod-hopping coppers calling would be bad enough; three—? Bassett and Bob made for the farmhouse, to a side door and sounds of muted voices.

Gumboots outside, workers inside. They glimpsed rolled-up shirtsleeves, green quilted chest-warmers, and—must be old Mr Boon, the farmer—a pair of old-fashioned braces. Farmer and men were on their feet, remains of a bread and cheese meal on the table, talk desultory, when Bob raised knuckles to knock.

Colin Bryan came to the door, Ken Collier at his shoulder. Both recognized Bassett, cast puzzled looks at Bob. 'We meet again,' Ken said to Bassett.

Bassett touched his hat. 'Mr Collier, Mr Bryan, this is Inspector Greenaway. Sorry to trouble you but we're still working on the Datsun case; like to ask one or two questions about Saturday.'

'Saturday? What are they on about, Colin?' The old man, out of sight now behind the door.

'Police, Dad, about that car.'

'The murder, you mean.' Mr Boon showed himself. 'Nasty business,' he said sorrowfully. 'I can't help you though, I know nowt. So I'm teking meself off if it's all the same to you. These two know nowt either, tek it from me. Lost my wife last Saturday, you know.'

'You'd best come in,' Colin Bryan said, as the old man shuffled off through a doorway on the far side of the kitchen.

It was a typical farmhouse kitchen: red-tiled floor, scrub-top table, dresser with blue-and-white chinaware aplenty, a grandfather clock; and a gun rack.

'We dislike having to bother you,' Bob Greenaway apologized. 'We'll be as brief as we can. We're busy checking the dead man's movements last Saturday. We have two witnesses who claim to have seen the Datsun heading slowly in this direction as if the driver were lost. We know he was a stranger to this area, and the address he had come to visit isn't the easiest to find. We wondered if he'd come here seeking directions.'

Colin Bryan shook his head, glanced questioningly at Ken Collier. 'What time are we talking about?' Ken asked the policeman.

'Say ten a.m. to ten-thirty.'

'The doctor hadn't long gone.' Ken addressed Colin. 'We'd have been in here, wouldn't we? If he'd come here we'd all have seen him,' he told the policemen. 'That's me, my wife, Colin here, and Mr Boon.'

'There was a tractor,' Bob Greenaway said. 'Who would have been working that?'

'Me.' Colin Bryan. The tractor was unattended, he said. He had been ditch-draining, the tractor was stationary, working the pump. And just in case they wondered why the noisy thing was pumping while Mrs Boon lay dying, as someone else had already pointed out to them, 'The last thing Maudie would have wanted would be a sickbed silence. Besides, the sound of the tractor might have brought her out of her stroke. It wasn't all that noisy anyway, not much more than a tickover.'

'But she didn't rally, alas.' Bassett, feelingly.

No, Maude Boon died on Saturday morning. Which was why they were all in the kitchen. The doctor had been and gone, they were all a bit numb, drinking tea to help pull themselves together. 'What else do you do after someone's died?' Ken Collier said solemnly. 'You don't remember the time you did everything for a start. But ten to ten-thirty, Colin.' He gazed inquiringly at his workmate. 'I'd have been dealing with phone calls for part of that time.'

Memory had been jogged. 'You would. You'd have been at home. Ken did the running about,' Colin told the policemen.

Bassett: 'You went home, Mr Collier?'

'To make phone calls, yes. So's the old man wouldn't hear. He was feeling it.'

'Home,' Bassett said. 'You are sure of the time?'

Ken said he was. 'I made some calls from the farm in the afternoon while Mr Boon had a sleep, the urgent calls, though—undertaker, vicar—I made from my house.' He glanced at the clock. 'Wait a minute.' Switched his gaze to Colin. 'The doctor came *downstairs* at ten o'clock.'

His workmate nodded. 'He was waiting for the clock to chime, fascinated him.'

'And then we talked. The district nurse was due at eleven to help Megan with Mrs Boon. She wasn't needed, the doctor said he'd let her know. And he was concerned for Megan, said she must catch up on some sleep. Aye; it must have been a quarter past when he finally left.'

'Is this Dr Lloyd?' Bassett said, guessing.

'No. Dr Hyde.'

Bassett took out his notebook. 'What then?'

'I followed the doctor out,' Colin told him. 'Pulled the plug on the tractor.'

'I had five minutes with Megan,' Ken said, 'then I went home to make the calls. Now I think about it—aye—it was a minute or two off half past ten when I got in. I remember now; it took three attempts to get through to the undertakers and I was beginning to sweat a bit, I had to get to the doctor's surgery in town before midday for the death certificate.'

'Did you manage it?' Bassett asked kindly.

'Mrs Mulholland went for me.'

'*Mrs Mulholland?*' Bob Greenaway's question.

'Yes. She'd seen the doctor leaving, and came to inquire about Mrs Boon.'

'She knew Mrs Boon was ill?' Bassett again.

'She'd have known within an hour of the old lady having her stroke, she has her own private radar, I think.' Ken

smiled. 'Give credit though, she offered to go to the surgery
for me, and came again later in the day to see if we needed
help with anything.'

'Don't mean to be rude,' Bassett said, 'but why would
she go to your house and not here, the farm.'

Ken shrugged. 'The old man. She'd crossed swords with
him more than once.'

'And she arrived at your house at what time?'

'Ohh.' A think. 'When? Quarter to eleven? Somewhere
round that time.'

Bassett turned to Colin Bryan. 'When the doctor left,
which way did he go?'

'I think along Cooper's Lane.'

Cooper's Lane: at around 10.15: either just before or just
after Kathy left with Alice. Where was Philip Read at that
time?

'You said Mrs Mulholland fetched the death certificate,
Mr Collier. She came again in the afternoon. Was that when
she brought the certificate?'

'No, she came straight back with it. The afternoon was a
separate visit.'

'So; she was at your house at ten forty-five a.m., went to
town, arrived back at what time?'

'Around midday.'

'She stay long?'

'Megan had come home to change into a grey frock. Mrs
Mulholland stayed and had a cup of coffee with her. Be one
o'clock when she left in the end.'

'Tied up for most of the morning,' Bassett murmured.
'What did you do after the phone calls, Mr Collier?'

'Came back here to tell Coll and Megan the undertaker
was sending someone to do the laying-out. Then I went
with Megan while she washed and changed . . . I didn't see
the Datsun. Not till late on Saturday afternoon. In the
lay-by it was then, and I thought nothing of it. I don't
suppose it registered till I'd seen it a couple more times.'

'Is it very important?' Colin Bryan asked.

'It would have helped perhaps if we'd found someone who recollected seeing him,' Bassett replied. 'We have no idea what time he arrived at the lay-by.'

'Droppers-by,' Bob Greenaway prompted. 'Anyone who would have come that way—?'

In the morning only the vicar, they said; it was afternoon before they saw anyone else, after Mrs Mulholland had spread the word.

'That seems to be it, then.' Bassett moved to go; halted. 'Might as well ask about the other while we're here, Bob, d'you think?'

'Why not? If you gentlemen don't mind. Plastic rubbish bags, Mr Bryan. You took two to the Bring and Buy. They were from here?'

'Mrs Boon's, yes, some of her things. Well, they were and they weren't.' Colin explained that Mrs Boon's sister had died some months previously. A niece had sent some of the sister's belongings to Mrs Boon thinking she might like them. Mrs Boon hadn't wanted them, so she had begged the items and stored them in her bedroom, to send them to a jumble sale after a decent interval.'

'In her bedroom,' Bassett said.

'Till Saturday. When Maude—Mrs Boon—died Mr Boon told me to get rid of them. I think he thought they'd brought bad luck.'

'So you removed them.' Still Bassett.

'I brought them down, put them outside—'

'And I took them across and put them in my shed,' Ken Collier said. 'Took them when I went to make the phone calls.'

'They remained in the shed until today?' Bob Greenaway spoke the question, then turned to Colin. 'Would you tell us exactly what you did when you got the bags from the shed this morning, Mr Bryan.'

He frowned. 'Is something wrong? They were only two

bags of old clothes . . . But all right, half way through the morning I thought of the pot-pourri. Mrs Boon was proud of her pot-pourri, we'd have been letting her down if we'd forgotten it. I went to Ken's with it . . .' He'd left it till late, he said, as he knew Megan had gone to town, wouldn't be back till after eleven. She would take the pot-pourri with her to the sale. She had just got in, they talked, Megan had a box of magazines to go, and they had decided between them that the bags might as well go as well. 'It was too much for Megan to maul about, so I loaded the lot into the Range-Rover and told her I'd deliver them to the hall for her. Which I did. Ken wasn't here to do it.'

'I'd forgotten all about the bags,' Ken said. 'I'd gone to Hereford on an errand for Mr Boon.'

Bob Greenaway nodded. He noticed Bassett studying both men. 'It was Mrs Collier's idea to take the bags, Mr Bryan.'

'No. She said she wondered if the bags ought to go. We discussed it, and, as I said, decided the things might as well do a bit of good as sit in the shed for mice to nibble at. I told her Maude would've agreed.'

'So it was more your idea than Mrs Collier's.'

'I—well, yes. Although the old man had said something about it after the funeral.'

The briefest pause; then Bassett said, 'What time did you get back from Hereford, Mr Collier?'

'Half past two, thereabouts.'

'Mr Bryan, which did you load into the Range-Rover first, the box or the bags?'

'Oh, blimey. Let me think. I went to the shed with Megan. She had the key, the shed was locked. I took the bags out, stood them by the Range-Rover while she locked up. She'd put the kettle on, she said. I might as well have a cuppa with her. I left the bags where they were, went into the house. Left, taking the pot-pourri. She called me back—what about the box of books? She took the pot-pourri and put it in one of the bags, I fetched the box. Box in first, the bags second and third . . . I don't understand any of this—'

Over to Bob Greenaway. 'The reason we ask, gentlemen—a doll we believe was stolen from the Datsun found its way to the village hall. Without going into detail, we suspect it got there in one of those bags.'

'That's ridiculous!' The soft explosion was from Ken Collier.

'Maybe not,' Bob said. 'We've just heard Mr Bryan say he left the bags by the Range-Rover while he went and had a cuppa—'

'Ten minutes?' Colin said. 'Someone messed with the bags while I was drinking a cup of tea? I can't see it.'

'No, neither can I on second thoughts,' Bob said, shaking his head. 'The someone would have had to be passing at the precise moment. Not likely, is it?'

'When was the man killed, *was* it Saturday?' Ken Collier sounded mildly stimulated. 'When I said I put the bags in the shed—I did, but not immediately. They were standing in the lean-to for most of the weekend. We call it a lean-to, it's just a small covered passage really, at the side of the house. We keep the dustbin in there, the wife's pot plants, odds and sods.'

Could it be seen from the road?

It could. 'And I saw old lady Meddlar on Saturday morning when I was going home with Megan for her wash and change. Saw her in the distance at the top of the road, but it couldn't have been anyone else wearing all the colours of the rainbow—' He broke off with a sheepish grin. 'Forget it. We were at home for the next hour. If she'd ventured near we'd have seen her.'

'Good try, Mr Collier,' Bassett said inoffensively.

Bob Greenaway turned to Colin Bryan. 'For the record, Mr Bryan, if someone had put the doll in one of the bags would you, could you, have seen or felt it? Felt it when you were carrying the bag?'

'I doubt it. A bag of stuff's a bag of stuff.'

'When you got to the village hall—?'

'Clem helped me unload them. I carried the bags, he took the box of books. Clem from Bletch House. I stood the bags on the floor where they were wanted, and helped him to pick up the books. The bottom fell out of the box as we entered the hall.'

'Ah.' Bassett smiled lightly. 'That happened inside. He was in your view the whole time.'

'We were together the whole time.'

Bassett smiled. 'That seems clear enough.'

No further questions. 'Thank you again, gentlemen,' Bob Greenaway said. A moment, and Bassett threw a glance at the gun rack. 'Do much shooting?'

They all did. 'Which is not to say we all hit what we're aiming at,' Ken Collier said, a grin forming. 'Colin here is a better shot with one eye than I'll ever be with two.'

He feinted a few friendly blows at Colin. Bob Greenaway and Bassett looked on, amused; then departed.

'The doctor left at 10.15 a.m.,' Bassett said as they moved out of earshot. 'Kathy left the Meddlars at roughly the same time. Presumably they missed one another. Philip Read passed Cooper's Lane turn-off at 10.00 a.m., was nowhere in sight at 10.15—doctor's corroboration would be useful— so question is: Where was he between 10.00 and 10.15 a.m.?'

Andy Miller caught up with them. 'Andy,' Bassett said cajolingly, 'you're doing a great job.'

Andy raised his eyes heavenwards. 'What do you want?' He grinned.

'Take the car to the lay-by, stop for a second, then drive on a distance to turn round. Want to see if the Datsun could have been seen from here.'

Answer: While it was in the lay-by, no, it could not. But the doctor's car driving along Cooper's Lane could have been seen by Colin Bryan while he was fiddling with the tractor.

'What does it prove?' Andy said, when he joined them again.

'Very little at the moment, Andy.' Bassett made a face at the young sergeant and Bob Greenaway. 'If Read didn't come to the farm, wasn't tucked in out of Kathy's view on Collier's driveway, perhaps he simply drove past the farm— the tractor was unattended, so why stop—and went on looking for another turn-off.'

'Towards Lymock,' Andy observed.

They didn't go searching, however. Bassett did that on his own after they had delivered him back to his Citroën. Bob and Andy made their priority a visit to Mrs Boon's doctor, Dr Hyde.

CHAPTER 20

'I don't think the doll was sneaked into the village hall after all,' Bassett told his reflection in his shaving mirror. 'I think it maybe did arrive there by accident. I think someone was going to try and smuggle it *out*.'

Pup listened attentively, big brown intelligent eyes following Bassett's every movement, tail thrashing the floor as always at the sound of his voice. He looked down at her. 'What say you, Babydog? To sneak something in when only you could've done so would be crazy. Best time would be when the place was packed. Put doll on table, woman at your elbow says: Oh! what a lovely doll! How much? Not priced. Busy server says: Well what do you offer? A pound? Yours for a pound. Done.' Even if a fuss had followed, its true worth noted, the first person seen handling the doll had simply to say she had picked it up to look at it. Hellish difficult to prove different. 'Agreed, Babydog?'

Agreed. Patiently. A shave usually signified an outing . . . An outing there would be: Friday night was Bassett's night for socializing at the Pheasant. He had asked Jack to bring gipsy Daniel Smith along: he wanted Daniel's description of the man in Bletch Heath pub last Tuesday who had called Robby a 'mad bugger'. Was it Clem, Colin Bryan, or Ken Collier?

There remained that other answer, too. The answer to: Did Robby have a nanny? Daniel had thought not; but he had promised to make inquiries.

Was the question still relevant? No matter. The question having been asked, Bassett would like to know the answer if only for elimination purposes.

Bassett's thoughts roamed on. The doll had almost certainly arrived at the Bring and Buy in one of Mrs Boon's black bags. Philip Read had almost certainly been killed because of—say a dark secret in somebody's past. Megan Collier had almost certainly lied about seeing the doll on the chair. And for a mother-to-be, expecting the baby she had been trying for for fifteen years, she was incredibly lack-lustre: where was the light of love in her eyes, the bloom on her cheeks, the *glow*? . . . But who knew of Philip Read's intended visit to the Meddlars? Annette Gray knew. Wasn't it Philip who telephoned while Pam Brown was there having coffee. And hadn't Annette gone out for half an hour afterwards?

Bassett had meditated on this while having his tea. The half an hour was a stumbling-block. Annette Gray was no fool: to go out, kill a man, and return immediately made little sense. Where was her alibi? All right, say she got blood on her clothes, had to get home to change them—wouldn't she then have gone out again, her story being, if asked, that she forgot her cheque-book or somesuch and had to go back for it? Wouldn't she have done something to cover her tracks?

Perhaps she had, in a way, belatedly. If her sister, Mrs Mulholland, was one of those people who talk about every house they enter; if Annette had gone ostensibly to offer her services to the bereaved, including Megan . . .

Megan again. Megan's house. The bags in their lean-to. Et cetera, et cetera. No clarity, no link yet. Except very loosely: Megan babysat for people who lived across the road from Annette; Megan had a faint Birmingham accent; Annette had been a nanny in Birmingham . . . But how long ago, for heaven's sake? Before Annette was married. Many moons ago.

Megan. Annette. Disjointed thoughts came and went. Were they disjointed? He relinquished the disjointed thoughts in favour of another.

Mrs Read had told Bob Greenaway that her husband had bought the doll for her. Had she volunteered the infor-

mation? Or had Bob told her what the shopkeeper said—
and Mrs Read simply agreed?

Suppose Philip Read had in fact bought the doll for
Annette . . . and suppose the telephone call had been or
contained a cryptic message . . .

That would mean they weren't the strangers Annette
maintained they were. Ergo, she wouldn't have killed him
for fear of being recognized . . . Ergo, they must look for an
alternative motive.

Not this evening, however.

Shaving tackle tidied away. Jollity in the air. 'Best bib
and tucker on now, Babydog!' Hat, walking stick, flashlamp,
raincoat as an afterthought in case it rained . . . 'We're on
our way!'

Raincoat . . .

Bassett mulled on while they walked the lanes. He knew
now what Philip Read had been doing between 10.00 a.m.
and 10.15 last Saturday. He *had* driven on past the farm.
Bassett had spoken to a teenager, a helpful young lad, who
recalled his mother speaking to a man who said he was
looking for Cooper's Lane. The mother had been expecting
a taxi to take her to the railway station; she'd heard a car
coming and had gone to the gate to wave him down, their
cottage having no name or number on the gate. It hadn't
been the taxi. The lad hadn't seen the man's car himself,
but: 'Mum will be back tonight, if you want to phone her
in the morning . . .'

Bassett would telephone her: in the meantime he believed
the lad, Read's being there slid neatly into the time slot.

Philip Read was on the Lymock Road at around 10.15
a.m. . . . Colin Bryan switched off the tractor, returned to
the farmhouse . . . Ken Collier had 'five minutes with
Megan', then went home to make telephone calls. To the
vicar and the undertaker—making a meal of it—couldn't
get through, he said. Collier's third task had been to go to
town for the death certificate. 'I was beginning to sweat a

bit,'—because he had to get there before noon . . . Mrs
Mulholland removed that burden when she arrived at
10.45 a.m., leaving him free to persevere with the telephone. When Mrs Mulholland returned, at midday,
Megan was with him . . .

Bassett's musings faltered, flipped a backward somer-
sault. 10.45. There was a gap there, surely. 10.45. *A quarter
to eleven*. He raked his memory . . . Yes . . . Yes . . . 10.45
a.m. for heaven's sake.

'Hope Reverend Willy hasn't deserted us in favour of
Bletch Heath tonight,' he muttered. 'Need to ask him about
Ken Collier's telephone call last Saturday.'

This Saturday, the following morning, dawned drizzly.
But 'Rain before seven, shine at eleven' had been a pet
saying of Mary's, and so with some of her optimism Bassett
completed his workaday chores, then sat down with notebook, pen and pipe to do some sorting out in the meantime.

So many notes. So many questions requiring to be
answered. Some he had dealt with, however.

Had Robby had a nanny? Answer: no. So, no known link
between Annette Gray and the Meddlars . . . Who called
Robby 'a mad bugger'? Answer: Chap with a plait. That is,
Ken Collier. Underline that.

Where was Philip Read between 10.00 a.m. and 10.15?
The teenager's mother had been on to the police station
very early, as much to clear the worry of concealing, or
rather withholding, useful information off her chest as to be
helpful. Helpful she had been, all the same. Andy Miller
had passed the information on to him. 'A bit after ten
o'clock, guvnor. Yellow car. Sounds like the Datsun. Looking for Cooper's Lane. Last she saw of him he'd turned the
car round just above her place and was standing by the
bonnet having a drink from a Thermos flask.'

He'd had a word with Doc McPherson, Andy said. Biscuit
in Philip Read's stomach, digestion hardly started, so time

of death virtually as per previous estimation. Instead of
between 10.00 a.m. and 11.00 make it 10.30 to 11.30, and
bear in mind that death had not been instantaneous, the
man had lived for some minutes after being attacked. Time
of attack could have been before 10.30 a.m.

And the question put to Reverend Willy, who hadn't
deserted his friends at the Pheasant? Willy confirmed that
his line had been busy last Saturday. Between the times
Bassett mentioned he couldn't swear to; but no vagueness
about Ken Collier's call, partly because of the nature of the
call, partly a remark Ken made towards the end of the
call—Mrs Mulholland had just walked in. Time of call?
Nearer five to eleven than a quarter to. Willy remembered
looking at the clock in order to tell Ken what time to expect
him at the farm.

The gap remained and had been widened.

Bassett jotted down an extra note or two, smoked a
thinking pipe; and half an hour later—the sun was shining—set off for Bletch Heath village shop.

'Mrs Arthur! Lovely day!'

'It is now. I love to see the sun, Mr Bassett.'

'So do I, Mrs Arthur.' Put a spring in his step.

She was wrapping up a parcel, had one end neatly folded.
'Carry on,' Bassett said, 'I only came to ask if Mrs Mulholland came into the shop last Saturday morning.'

'Olivia? No. Annette did. She came in for some knitting
wool. I don't keep a large stock but she found some she
liked.'

Bassett ran his eyes along the shelves. 'Baby wool?'

'Baby wool?' Whatever gave him that idea! 'No. Some of
that nice mulberry at the end there.'

'Oh.' Bassett mocked himself. 'Thought she was going to
knit rompers or a bonnet for Megan Collier.'

'She might be,' Joan Arthur said effusively, 'but she had
no baby wool from me.'

Bassett lingered, watching her. 'Can I give you a hand with that?'

'Would you?' She laughed. 'I'm hopeless with Sellotape.'

'Me too. Get into a terrible mess. Ends up in me hair, up me arms, on the dog, down in the hen pen—'

She laughed. Thought he was joking.

He continued chattily. 'I'm going to have a look-see at one or two rest homes—'

'For Alice?'

'Well . . .' Non-committally. 'Which one is the relation in? Not Rosemead . . .'

'No, the other one not far from you. I remembered it after you'd gone the other day. Garland House. The relation's name is Thea. *That* I never forget, I thought it was short for Theodora, same as an aunt of mine. It isn't though, it's short for Dorothea.'

'Thea,' Bassett repeated. The name was what he had wanted. 'And Annette was here at half past eleven last Saturday.'

'Oh no, it wasn't that late. More like ten o'clock. Des had his coat on. He'd got an appointment in town at ten-thirty. He left while Annette was here. I think you'll find Olivia was at Boon's Farm all Saturday morning—doing her bit, as she puts it . . . Oh, that's smashing,' she said gratefully. 'Best parcel I've done up in ages, thanks to you! Sure I can't get you anything?'

'I might as well have some tobacco while I'm here. Annette here long?'

'Matter of fact, no. I said take your time with the wool, but she knew what she wanted before she came in. Said she was in a bit of a hurry, she was half expecting a visitor. Anything wrong? I—'

'No, no,' Bassett said, smiling. 'The Datsun, we're still trying to track its movements. Scarcely anyone seems to have seen it.'

'Well, not many people use Cooper's Lane, do they?

Easier to go the other way round to Glevebourne and that
. . . Talking of visitors,' Joan Arthur said perkily as she
waited for Bassett's money, 'I'm off to see Alice this afternoon. I rang up, they said I could go. I don't suppose the
poor love will have had many go to see her.'

'No, I don't suppose she will. Does she eat chocolate?
Take her a box of those, will you? Tell her they're from
Robby.'

''Morning!' She sang it at the top of a loud voice, caused a
gale-force wind to blow as she swept past him, wafting fresh
air and perfume in her wake, and called over her shoulder,
'Can't stop. Important meeting!'

'Olivia?' he said a moment later, to Annette, who had
seen him coming and was waiting on the step.

'Olivia,' she replied with an amused smile.

'Handsome woman.' For all her size.

'She wears me out.' Not complainingly, however. 'She's
going to see Eileen Read. And I'm going to put my feet up
for the rest of the day. I think I've a cold coming on.' A
mischievous look. 'I hope it's a cold, not Pam's boys' measles.'

'Oh dear.' Bassett commiserated. She did have dark
shadows around her eyes, and she was hugging herself inside
a large paisley shawl. And she did smell of eucalyptus.
'Perhaps I'd better let you get off to bed with your hot
lemon.'

Waved away graciously. 'I've made myself a nest in the
sitting-room. If you don't mind my germs . . .'

He didn't. Cosy room. The room of someone clever with
her fingers: homemade rugs, tapestry footstool and cushions;
knitting at one end of the sofa. 'Sit down, Mr Bassett.'

He chose an armchair, she the sofa. 'I won't beat about
the bush, Mrs Gray. I know that Mr Read spoke to you on
the telephone last Saturday morning.'

'Yes, he did.'

'If memory serves, you told me you had never met the

man, that he and his wife were Olivia's friends, not yours.'

'Perfectly true. He phoned us—Olivia and me. It so happened that I answered the telephone. He wanted to know the location of a particular shop.'

'Did he tell you why he wanted that particular shop?'

'No.' And when Bassett made it clear he wanted more, 'He said he was in Glevebourne, would be going on to the Meddlar place, and, depending on how long he spent with them, might stop by and tell Olivia how he got on.'

'You passed the message on to Olivia.'

'In due course, yes.'

'She didn't wait for him, she went out.'

'Yes.' She caught a sneeze in a handkerchief. 'I was in the hall with Pam—from across the road—when Philip phoned. Olivia was in the kitchen. I had no intention of discussing the call in front of Pam, or of going into the kitchen and shutting the door on her while I passed the message on. Unfortunately Pam can be very talkative. We were still talking when Olivia decided to go to the library. I told her when she got back.'

'Which would have been after one o'clock.'

'Yes. Too late to expect him then. I told her what he'd said, and that no doubt he'd be in touch.'

'What did she say?'

'Oh . . .' She was about to say something like 'Nothing of any consequence' if her mouth was anything to go by; changed her mind. 'She was a little annoyed. With Eileen. Eileen had said nothing to her about bringing Philip into it, she said. But she didn't make an issue of it, she told me about Mrs Boon's death and old Mr Boon's distress.'

'She'd found another worry,' Bassett said lightly, referring to a previous conversation. 'And of course Olivia had never met Philip Read, didn't you say?'

'No, she hadn't. I believe she was friends with Eileen before Eileen and Philip married. I have to confess I don't know my sister very well. There's a big age gap. I was only

nine when she married Paddy Hill, her first husband. We
lived our own, different lives for many years. We started
seeing each other when I worked in Birmingham—she
lived in Wolverhampton, a bus ride away,' Annette continued reminiscently. 'It was rather nice having an older
sister for a while.' She gave Bassett a reserved smile. 'Then
I moved on. Paddy was killed in a road accident and Olivia
moved on . . . She married Bertie Mulholland about ten
years ago. He was in business in Dudley, did a lot of work
for charity. That was how Olivia came to be involved with
voluntary work, and how she met Eileen, I imagine.'

'And you, Mrs Gray.' Warmly. 'What kind of life did you
have?'

'A very good life, Mr Bassett. My Ted was one of the
best. We had some wonderful times together. Ted was a
civil engineer. Bridges, viaducts, beautiful structures. We
travelled, met interesting people.' She left it there: fond
memories.

'Olivia lived in Scotland for a time.'

'After Bertie died. She went to stay with his uncle, the
one she visits every year. I was on my own too shortly
afterwards, I spent some months with them. I've probably
seen more of Olivia in the past four years than during the
rest of our lives put together. I couldn't stand Scottish
winters though, so there was never any question of my
making a home there. I prefer it down here where it's
warmer. Olivia came to live with me.'

'To move on again soon,' Bassett said.

'This job of hers? It would seem so.'

'With Eileen Read, isn't it? The home Eileen is planning
to open.'

'How on earth do you know that?' Annette frowned.

A calculated guess.

'She didn't tell me, you know.' The furrows in her forehead evening out. 'Not until today. She told me about the
job when she telephoned from Scotland. Told me that was

why she went on the spur of the moment—she wanted to get the visit over so that she would be free of encumbrances for several months. But I only knew about Eileen and the rest home today. She's so excited, I hope it doesn't fall through.

'Is that a possibility?'

'I don't know. It might be now that Philip is no more. Apparently it was mainly for his sake that the idea took root. OAPs on the increase. Homes for them a growing industry. Philip wanted to pack in his job and write. He and Eileen were to carry on working for two years with a manager running the home until it was established, then Eileen would gradually take it over, leaving Philip free.'

Bassett acknowledged with a slow nod. Annette sneezed into her handkerchief several times in quick succession, laughed it off with a nasal, 'I hate colds.'

'Can I get you anything?' Bassett said solicitously. 'I'm going to Glevebourne, could pop into a chemist's.'

'Good of you, but not necessary, I assure you.'

Then he would leave her in peace. 'Just one thing, Mrs Gray. I'm puzzled about why you were so surprised the other morning—when I told you it was Philip Read who was missing, not Eileen.'

'I can't remember that I was surprised,' she said. 'I was *confused*. I didn't connect a yellow Datsun with Philip and Saturday until much later, after I'd thought about it. I had only ever seen Eileen with the Datsun.'

Made sense, Bassett had to admit. He didn't stop her when she got up to show him out: something he had noticed in the hall.

'My wife had a raincoat this colour,' he fibbed, pausing at the coat-rack. 'Her favourite colour, old rose pink. Yours?'

'No, that's Olivia's. Mine is the green.'

Annette Gray stood for some seconds in the hall after Bassett had gone, holding her feverish cheeks between both hands. After a while she went to the raincoats and sniffed them, trying to detect cleaning fluid smells. Thank God! they both smelt more or less the same.

CHAPTER 21

There was a public telephone kiosk on the road to Garland House. Bassett drew up, dialled the number of Glevebourne Police Station; spoke to Bob Greenaway.

'Bob, photographs of the doll. Can you get me half a dozen glossy prints?'

'No problem. Pick them up from the front desk. Are you on to something?'

'I may be. I'll let you know.'

Garland House, 'Home for the Elderly and Convalescent', stood surrounded by woodland, with its own lake, walks, gardens. An old three-storey building refurbished, its modern reception area included tasteful tables for four, flowers on every table, and a small kitchen where drinks could be made. When Bassett arrived a young family and their grandmother were enjoying coffee and buns. Fun in the air. He was impressed. If only all homes for the elderly could be like this! No reason why they shouldn't be when you thought about it.

The blonde-haired, unobtrusive receptionist wore a dark suit, crisp blouse, pearls, and genuine smile.

'Name's Bassett. May I see Thea, please? I'm afraid I don't know her surname.'

'Mrs Ward.' The receptionist beamed. 'I'll see if she's free.'

While she did something with a telephone Bassett looked around for the source of a not-unfriendly argument taking place: over a bird among the primulas, one voice insisting it was a young blackbird, the other that it was a thrush. A white-haired couple dressed for outdoors stopped to speak.

'Are you joining us? If you need help with your suitcase John will help you, won't you, John?' John said he would be delighted. 'D'you play bridge, old man? Rubber most evenings.'

Bassett grinned fatuously. Saved. The receptionist advised Bassett that Mrs Ward would see him now. He waved the couple off. 'Nice meeting you!' And was directed to a door round the corner.

Ah. The door was marked 'Mrs Ward' but the room was no bed-sitting-room, it was an office.

'I appear to have made a boo-boo,' Bassett said with little loss of composure. 'I'm looking for a lady named Thea related to an Olivia and Annette.'

'You've found her. I'm their cousin. Come in and sit down.' The tone was welcoming, the chuckle intended to put him at ease. 'You thought I was an oldie?'

'Are you allowed to say that—oldie?'

'We are. Common sense reigns here. We are a lot of creaking bones, swollen joints, false teeth and hairpieces, and other unmentionable symptoms of old age, but that doesn't mean we are decrepit. We sympathize with each other, or not as the case may be, and get on with enjoying life. Being old doesn't have to mean the end of everything. End of lecture!'

Bassett gave grin for grin. 'I may put me name down while I'm here.'

'Why not? For the year 2000? I must warn you, though, that we do have our downs as well as ups, not all is perfection!'

To business. 'I'm a retired superintendent of police, Mrs Ward, working on a case in a private capacity. This conversation is therefore confidential.'

Understood.

He improvised. 'I'm in the awkward position of requiring information about your cousins in order to eliminate them from inquiries. I'm hoping that you can assist me. Do you know if either of them has ever needed help from a social services department?'

'In what way?' She eyed him with vague suspicion. 'You're not investigating fraudulent claims—?'

'I wasn't thinking of financial help.'

'No, and I don't honestly believe they ever had any. What else? Olivia's first husband was a gambler, they were down to a knife, fork and spoon apiece many a time. But it never lasted for long, he'd win all back again the following week, so to speak.'

'Was he ever in trouble with the law?'

'I'm sure not. Just as I'm sure Olivia wouldn't have sought refuge or re-housing or anything of that nature. She thought the world of him, wouldn't hear a word against her beloved Paddy. Her second husband died penniless; he'd struggled on with an ailing business when he should have sold up and got out. Assets cleared his debts, though, and Olivia went to live with his uncle in Scotland. She wasn't broke, she had Bertie's insurance money. And they had been happy as far as I am aware.'

'Any children?'

'Olivia had no liking for children. Annette was the one who loved children, which is why she became a children's nanny.'

'She had none of her own,' Bassett probed gently.

'Sadly, she couldn't. After three miscarriages she decided that nature was trying to tell her something. She and Ted accepted childlessness.'

'Girls who become nurses often do so after spending time in hospital themselves, or after nursing a sick relation,' Bassett said. 'Is it possible that Annette chose to be a nanny because of a child in her life? Is it possible that she had a child when she was very young, still at school for instance?'

'Quite impossible,' Cousin Thea said. 'We were at school together, left together. Annette went to be trained as a nanny, I did nurse training.'

Bassett nodded to himself. Exit the notion he'd had that
Megan from an orphanage might be the daughter of Annette
Gray.

'There was the stealing,' Thea said tentatively. 'It happened so long ago I can't see how it could possibly affect
an inquiry now, but—'

'*Stealing.*' Bassett's pulse thumped an extra beat. 'What
was that about?' he said equably.

'It could have ruined Annette's life if it hadn't been for
Ted . . .'

'Ted Gray, the man she married.'

'Yes. Annette had a super position in Birmingham after
she finished her training. She was as happy as I had ever
known her be. Until the stealing came to a head. Annette
swore her innocence; she told me in confidence that she
thought the thief was Olivia, that Olivia was a kleptomaniac, but she'd no proof. I went to see her employers.
They agreed that the thefts did appear to coincide with
dates on which Olivia had been at the house. They also
agreed not to prosecute, the items weren't of great value,
but poor old Annette was given notice. It broke her heart.
Not so much that she had to go, but that she went under a
cloud.'

'Where did Ted come in? He was a friend of her employers' wasn't he?'

'Yes, and they were unofficially engaged. They married
and he took her off to Cornwall . . . Is this of use to you?'

'Yes, Mrs Ward, I believe it is.'

How useful Bassett wasn't sure. Philip Read would have
been in short trousers when Annette Gray was sacked; yet
he was confident that somewhere amid what Cousin Thea
had told him lay the answer to the man's murder.

After leaving Garland House he sat in his car thinking.
It was nice having an older sister for a while, Annette had
said.

For a while. The siblings had become friends when Annette

worked in Birmingham. They had parted, one banished
in disgrace. Olivia had continued living in the West Midlands. In later years she had worked with Eileen Read.
Social worker Eileen.

Here Bassett's deliberations took a tumble: Olivia had
worked with Eileen Read. Worked with, not *been counselled by*.
They had lost touch, renewed the friendship after Eileen
Read's marriage. The picture postcard in his pocket told
him this. He took the card out and read it again. 'Remember
me? Eileen (Welling)? Married now . . . So happy I have
to tell the world! . . .' At the end a telephone number, and
'Love, Eileen.'

Bassett stared at the signature.

Stared, and lost himself in thought.

Yes. Yes, he had it! Time he spoke to Eileen.

He spoke to Eileen Read from a public telephone-box
in Glevebourne, explained who he was, and, 'I believe
Mrs Mulholland is on her way to you, otherwise I
should be asking if I might come and see you myself.
Would you mind answering me a question or two over the
phone?'

'If I can.'

'Who knew beforehand that your husband was going to
see Mrs Meddlar on Saturday, anyone?'

'No, no one,' was the reply. 'Unless Philip said something
in the office, which I doubt. Philip thought he was merely
doing me a favour.'

'You didn't take Mrs Mulholland's concern too much to
heart. Am I right?' Bassett said.

'Frankly, yes. I was reluctant to interfere. I had no
authority to do so.'

'And—?' Bassett said, sensing there was more on the tip
of Eileen's tongue.

'I took the view that if there had been room for concern
the people of Bletch Heath would have done something

about it themselves. In fact I asked Olivia who had tipped her off. No one had. My advice was for her to leave well alone, but she was so persistent I realized I'd get no peace until I at least made some kind of gesture . . . I discussed it with Philip, and he offered to see the Meddlars. Olivia was far more likely to listen to his findings than to mine . . . In a nutshell, Mr Bassett,' she said with a drawn-out sigh, 'Philip was going to get Olivia off my back.'

'You discussed it with your husband—when?'

'I had tea with Olivia and Annette on Tuesday, Tuesday before last. I was determined *not* to interfere until Thursday. I spoke to Philip about it on the Thursday evening, asked him what I should do. Friday lunch-time he volunteered to—as he put it—humour Olivia.'

'Friday was the day before—'

The day before Philip was murdered.

'He didn't say when he would go, he didn't know himself. Sometime over the weekend, when the mood was upon him,' Eileen Read said. 'Did you say Olivia was on her way to me?'

'According to Annette.'

'She still won't leave me alone . . . Oh, don't mind me, it's just that she clings so. And I don't particularly want to see her yet.'

'I think she's coming to discuss the job,' Bassett began slowly. He almost made it a question.

'There is no job.'

Bassett heard the frustration. No job now that Philip was dead, or—?

Eileen Read interrupted his thoughts. 'There's someone at the door, if you'll excuse me—'

Thinking this might be her way to get rid of him, Bassett cut in quickly, 'Mrs Read, I have to talk to you some more, if you could spare me the time. Will you be free this evening? Or tomorrow, Sunday?'

She considered. 'Tomorrow. I shall be coming to your part of the world tomorrow.'

They made arrangements.

The photographs weren't at the front desk. Instead a message awaited Bassett: Bob Greenaway wanted to see him. Deflated Bassett somewhat, he'd fancied he was the one with News. Seemed Bob was on the verge of success.

Bob was quietly excited. 'I think we're nearly there, Harry. Only scuttlebutt stuff so far, but it's beginning to tie in with your theory. The Colliers. They were hippies working the pop music circuit, and never made it. Been together for fourteen or fifteen years, married only four. Seems she was one of his groupies, had a couple of kiddies she dragged around with them until they were taken off her. Could be we have our motive. If Philip Read was one of their social workers—new life, new baby, past hidden— We're giving it everything we've got.'

'There's only one problem, Bob.'

'What's that?'

But Bassett shook his head. Let Bob carry on; Bob could be right, he wrong. He massaged his nose, poked fun at himself. 'I had another candidate lined up . . . Got those photos? I might as well follow it through, gives me something to do over the weekend.'

Bob Greenaway looked bemused.

'Weekend'll slow you down, won't it?' Bassett said, pausing at the door. 'Getting records and what-have-you. Mind if I look in on the Colliers? No use your going until you have something concrete.'

Bob Greenaway scowled. 'What are you up to?'

'Well if you're right, and I'm wrong—'

'OK. I haven't time to argue—'

Downstairs, Bassett spoke to the desk sergeant. 'Wilson in? Dabs Wilson?'

Not until Monday unless there was anything urgent.

'Give me his home number,' Bassett begged with a wink. 'Trust me. He won't find out where I got it.'

He then drove to Boon's Farm, there to hand one photograph to Colin Bryan—'Photograph of the doll, Mr Bryan. Have you seen it before?'—and another to old Mr Boon.

From the farm he went directly to the Colliers'.

CHAPTER 22

'You're a musician.' Bassett motioned towards the guitar on a chair in the hall.

'Aye, I've been practising a couple of numbers.' Ken Collier, wearing white silk shirt, smart corduroy trousers, and tan waistcoat, looked pleased by Bassett's interest. 'I'm playing at a wedding reception tonight. Bit of pocket money for Megan.'

Megan appeared in the doorway of an inner room. Bassett doffed his hat, said hello. 'I've come to beg a look at that lean-to of yours, Mrs Collier. First, if you could spare me a few minutes, I'd like another word about the doll.'

He was about to be shown into the best room, but the kitchen would do nicely, he said. 'I can smell a hot iron. Don't let me delay you. Carry on.' Keep it homely.

The ironing was finished: newly laundered clothes hung from a rack in a corner. 'Mr Bassett might like a cup of tea, Meggie, love.'

Mr Bassett would love one, perhaps in a minute or two.

'What's the problem?' Ken said cheerfully, drawing and holding a chair for Megan. He and Bassett perched on kitchen stools. 'It's about the doll, Meggie.'

Bassett nodded. 'The doll was stolen from the Datsun, Mrs Collier. Did your husband tell you? He did, good. When the doll turned up at the Bring and Buy Sale we assumed that the thief or a person known to the thief had decided to get rid of it by letting it be sold along with a hundred other items. As you know, if that was the plan, it failed . . . We have been trying to discover how the doll got to the Sale. We believe it arrived in one of Mrs Boon's bags of cast-off clothing. Colin Bryan took the bags to the Sale, he doesn't deny it . . . But that means, I'm afraid,

Mrs Collier, that when you claimed to have found the doll
on the chair you weren't speaking the truth.'

'I'm not with you.' Ken answered for his wife. 'Why
would Megan even mention it if it wasn't true?'

'I have wondered about that,' Bassett said, not unkindly.
'No one actually saw you with the doll, did they, Mrs
Collier? But you thought they might have. The two women
who entered the hall shortly after you said you were leaving
the sorting-table empty-handed. You said you had just put
the doll on the table. So, fine, the stories tally. But they also
said you looked guilty—as if you had been going to steal
something. We can take that with a pinch of salt—or we
can ask ourselves why you should be wearing a guilty
expression if all you had done was put a doll on a table
which you had found on a chair. Do you see what I'm
getting at?'

'I explained to that Inspector——' Megan's face had
brightened. 'I told him I'd been tempted to take the doll.
It was so pretty, and if we have a little girl—'

Bassett was shaking his head. 'No. We think you had just
taken it out of the bag. The doll *shouldn't* have gone to the
village hall, it *was* a mistake, as someone said at the time.
We think you had the task of retrieving it.'

'No . . .'

'We think that what you intended to do was put it with
your handbag and coat by your own table, and bring it
home with you at the end of the day. Everyone would be
loaded down with goodies by then, and you would have had
plenty of time to pack it into a large carrier bag, cover it up
with a bag of buns, a jar of chutney or two. Unfortunately,
as I say, you heard the two women coming. What should
you do—dash with it to your own table and risk being
caught in mid-flight? Or dump it? You dumped it on the
table nearest you—the sorting-table—dropped a woolly
garment on top of it, and told yourself you would whip it
away at the first opportunity.

'The opportunity was slow to come. In fact you lost out. Then came the fuss. You couldn't be sure how much or how little the women had seen, so to allay suspicion and cover yourself you cooked up the tale of having spotted the doll on a chair.'

A silence fell. Megan stared down at her hands in her lap. 'I didn't—that word you said—'

'Retrieve it.'

'I didn't know it was a mistake or anything. I did like it, I did want it, that was all.'

'I can understand that,' Bassett said. 'No one is blaming you. Now would you tell me what really happened?'

'Will I get into trouble?'

'Not if you tell the truth.'

'The doll was in the bag,' she said. 'I saw it after Coll had taken the bags out of the shed—when he went to get my box of books and I took the pot-pourri to put inside one of the bags. I'd never looked inside them. There was a blouse on top of the one I opened. It looked too pretty to go to a jumble sale, lace and everything. I half lifted it out to have a better look and saw the doll. Well, only one end of the box and its little feet really, it had been pushed down the middle of rolled-up skirts and things . . . I didn't like to rummage because Coll was coming, so I thought if I was first in after dinner I could have a proper look, and if it wasn't broken or anything I'd take it and no one would ever know it had been there.

'I did feel guilty when Anne and Betty, I mean Helga and Betty, came and nearly caught me. I knew they would think I was stealing it. Also, if they saw it I wouldn't be able to have it, someone would notice it was missing. So I did what you said—put it on the table. I thought Helga and Betty would go through to the kitchen, but they didn't, they seemed to be watching me all the time.'

'You are a Charlie,' husband Ken said affectionately. 'You could have got us both in trouble.' He looked at

Bassett. 'Still, all's well that ends well. The police won't be
too hard on her, will they?'

'Shouldn't think so.' Bassett smiled at Megan.
'You'll have to make another statement but you won't
mind that. And I wouldn't mind that cup of tea now, if I
may.'

'I'll make a fresh pot.'

Bassett turned to her husband. 'Could you and I have a
look at the lean-to?'

Outside, Bassett said loudly, 'I see you grow broad
beans . . .' and drew Ken towards them, away from the
kitchen door and open window.

'The problem now, Mr Collier, is how the doll got into
the bag in the first place. I'm going to be blunt and tell you
that at the moment you are prime suspect.'

'Me? The frown seemed to be the frown of innocence.

'You see,' Bassett said, 'we finally tracked down the
social worker's movements last Saturday. We know he
didn't call at the farm for directions; he went past the farm
and along the road towards Lymock. Found out what he
wanted to know—and would have been returning to pass
your house at around the time you were leaving the farm to
make those telephone calls to the undertaker and the vicar
. . . It's possible that he stopped, as I might have done, and
called to you: Am I on the right road now for Cooper's
Lane? It's possible that you recognized him, said: I'll come
with you, easier to show you than to tell you. Got your car
out, led the way, bashed him, drove home shaking, certainly
making a mess of the phone calls since you'd used up a
precious fifteen minutes or so, and were indeed "sweating
a bit" when Mrs Mulholland arrived.'

'No! What is this?'

'Of course it might not have been you he saw, it could
have been Colin—Colin tinkering with the tractor. Except
that we know Colin took the bags to the village hall. If Colin
killed Philip Read and hid the doll in the bag it would be

senseless of him to leave it in the bag with things which could identify where it came from—'

'Hold it! Hold it! You're saying I went with this bloke to the Meddlars', bashed him, stole his doll . . .' Ken Collier stared. 'You didn't believe Megan back there.'

'I believe she took the doll out of the bag.'

'Retrieve. That means get back. You think—!'

'What I think doesn't matter, Mr Collier. You do see what it looks like, though? The doll in the bag, the bag locked in your shed . . . you forgetting about the Bring and Buy.'

'What is that supposed to mean? You think I—you think I asked Megan—I was in Hereford till after two o'clock!'

'You could have telephoned her,' Bassett said calmly. 'Megan, love, I've this minute remembered it's your Bring and Buy. Don't take those two bags yet . . . They've already gone? Damn. Look, there's a doll inside one of them—'

'I don't believe I'm hearing this,' Ken Collier said with a nervous laugh. 'You're saying I went with this bloke, bashed him—'

'I'm saying it's possible.'

'And then I suppose I borrowed a spade from Mad Robby—'

'No. You left the body where it fell. After you had taken the car keys. You had to make sure there was nothing in the car to incriminate you. You had his briefcase, he'd been carrying that. You found the doll, couldn't resist taking it. Got home, for speed shoved the doll into one of Mrs Boon's bags—'

'And left the bag in the lean-to for the rest of the weekend, for anybody to have a nose in?' Ken scoffed.

'A precaution,' Bassett said. 'The murder could have been discovered at any time. A missing doll? People had been in and out of the farm all weekend; the lean-to can be seen from the road; if the doll were to have been found in the bag—anybody could have put it there. After the

weekend—well, who would think of looking here? You
locked the bags up in the shed; if luck was on your side now
the murder inquiry would be completed, the doll might not
even feature in it, and one day you would be free to make
a present of it to Megan.'

'This is crazy!' Alarm was showing. Alarm and—what?
A slow dawning? 'Who thought this out? Some copper take
a dislike to my hair? Or did they latch on to me because I
reported the Datsun? Yes—that's it, isn't it? They latched
on to me because of that, found out that I *could* have done
it—you've just proved how easy it would have been—and
it's me for the high jump.'

Bassett waited. In the periphery of his vision he saw Ken
Collier ball his fists. 'They've really got me sewn up!' Alarm
was being overtaken by anger. A good sign.

'What the hell are they making me out to be?' Ken Collier
cursed between clenched teeth. No raised tone, he was
sufficiently in control to have consideration for his pregnant
wife. 'A perfect stranger stops by my house—and I kill him.
What am I, for Christ's sake? A raving loony?'

'Was he a stranger?' Bassett asked levelly.

'How the hell do I know? I never met him! He could have
been my best friend—except that I never knew anybody by
the name of Read.' He swung on Bassett. 'Where do you fit
in? It wouldn't be you, would it, who—?'

'No. I'll be honest, Mr Collier, I did have you down for
it once. Do you remember our first meeting? We were talking
about Robby Meddlar and welfare people. You told me
your wife thought she had seen a health visitor going into
Mrs Mulholland's house. To explain why your wife thought
'health visitor' you added a district nurse bag. I fancied you
were being devious, getting your message across as best you
were able. I knew, you see, that the woman was Mrs Read,
who does similar work to her husband's—she's a social
worker.

'Then your wife told a friend that she thought the woman

was a nurse. Presumably a nurse in mufti. The picture was becoming muddled. The woman was not a health visitor, not a nurse, merely a woman in ordinary clothes. Yet she had attracted your wife's attention. Why? I decided there could be only one answer—your wife was attracted to the woman's face; she had seen the face before.

'A face from the past, Mr Collier? To do with children, I told myself. Why children? Small things. Your wife's wanting to keep secret the baby she had so badly yearned for fifteen years, she said. The happiness that wasn't there but should have been. A niece and nephew no one ever saw, save in a photograph.

'I built up a case against you. I imagined your wife becoming worried when she spotted Mrs Read. What if the woman hadn't turned up on account of Robby? What if that talk about welfare officers for Robby had been a ploy? . . . What if, when Mr Read called to you from the Datsun and said he was looking for the Meddlars, *you didn't believe him?* After all, only you called Robby a Mad Bugger. No one in Bletch Heath had ever called Robby that. It seemed to me that you said more about Robby *after* Mr Read's death than you had ever said before. Whoever killed Mr Read expected Robby to be blamed. You seemed to go out of your way to point the finger in his direction.'

'I was only repeating what Mrs Mulholland had been saying. And Mrs Gray—she ran out of the shop crying murder. I'm sorry if I went too far. But look where I live— nothing between their place and ours. And Megan having a baby. I was worried to death. If he ran amok . . . Or his mother with her shotgun.' He darted a glance. 'I heard he'd been arrested.'

'Taken into care while his mother is in hospital,' Bassett said.

'He's not under suspicion, I am. Why me?' The voice was hard now.

'The so-called niece and nephew,' Bassett said.

'It was a long time ago.'

'And you were young and irresponsible.'

'Not that irresponsible. The children were taken away from Megan, yes, but she—we weren't bad parents, they admitted it in the end . . . They were only little tots, and they loved their foster mum and dad. By the time we could have had them back they had forgotten us. We did what was best for them—we let their foster parents adopt them legally . . . But we can see them whenever we want. We're their Auntie Megan and Uncle Ken. We get photographs, send them Christmas presents. Where is a motive for murder in that?'

Bassett nodded. It sounded all right. 'Why was your wife worried to death when she saw Mrs Read?'

'Gossip. Tongues wagging. We're not proud of what we did. We've made a new start. How long would it last if it all came out? There are people who would never feel the same about us again, we'd be the lowest of the low for giving away our children.'

'Then let us hope they never do find out,' Bassett said.

Megan called to them: the tea was ready.

'Where do we go from here?' Ken Collier asked, as they left the vegetable garden to go to her.

'Nowhere,' Bassett replied. 'I shall be seeing Inspector Greenaway. Before I go I'll have a glance at your shotgun and licence. You do keep a shotgun in the house, not at the farm?'

'Yes . . .'

'Good.' Bassett smiled. 'I thought you might.'

CHAPTER 23

'So the children were adopted. There's still a pile of evidence piled up against the Colliers.'

'Circumstantial, Bob. We are agreed, are we not, that whoever killed Philip Read expected the Meddlars to be blamed for it. Ken Collier is familiar with the legend of Mrs Meddlar and her shotgun. He wouldn't have killed Read with a lump of wood—he'd have used his shotgun.'

Granted, Alice never used a live cartridge, but how many people knew that? And it would be nigh on impossible to fit a particular shotgun to a specific death.

Bassett knew the killer wasn't Kathy either. The day she had gone with him to flush Robby out she had rushed to point out that Alice wouldn't have fired her shotgun, the police would soon find that out. In other words Kathy had no idea how Philip Read died. She thought, as no doubt did others, that he had been shot to death.

Colin Bryan? He had a rough childhood, child abuse could have entered into it. But the man made no secret of the fact that he came from an unhappy home or that the Boons had taken him in. In short, as far as Bassett could tell, Colin Bryan had nothing to hide. He therefore had no reason to kill Philip Read.

And old Mr Boon? He could have a past, a brush with the law in another town, say; but he was too old for exposure to bother him now. Exposure to whom, anyhow? Who would he want to keep from learning about his disgrace? His wife? She had died that same morning. Who else was there?'

'Who did it, then?' Bob Greenaway asked. 'You must have someone lined up.'

'I have, Bob. I need a few more hours. Enjoy your Sunday, I'll contact you later.'

Sunday. A cool, slightly too breezy to be frosty morning; a morning—Bassett told pup—to set off on a brisk walk and blow the cobwebs away. He would have liked nothing better than to hike the six miles across-country to say hello to Kathy and her little 'un, and to lean on his walking stick, acting as foreman while Clem attended to Alice's chickens; but walking was time-consuming, he had told Bob he needed a few more hours, he must keep it to a few, which meant a busy day ahead.

His own hens and pup had to take priority: one of the joys of retirement was the freedom to put his own responsibilities first. So he fed his hens and cleaned out their nest-boxes, reminded Cocky to keep a beady on his girls; and took pup for a romp on her favourite hill.

From a high spot Bassett looked down across the valley, and turned a slow full circle surveying peaceful countryside in all directions.

Peaceful. Yet murder stalked.

He recalled a recent case he had worked on, and two sisters, one pretty, one plain: and tried to find similarities with today's two sisters, Olivia and Annette; found none, none that would help him at any rate, except in so far as where they had loved each other, those first two sisters, they had also hated. It was something he needed to remember well.

It was to Olivia and Annette he made his first visit of the day, arriving as they prepared to go to church.

'Won't keep you a moment, Mrs Gray, Mrs Mulholland. Have either of you ever seen this doll?' He gave each of them a photograph; on the back of one was a lightly pencilled O, on the other an A, and he himself handled them meticulously.

'Is this the famous doll? Eileen was telling me about

it,' was Olivia's over-bright response. Over-bright because Eileen had told her there was no job, Bassett asked himself, and she was putting on a brave face?

Gentle Annette, her cold having drained her face of its natural colour, caressed the doll with her eyes and handed the photograph back with a tiny headshake. No, sorry. And a small smile.

To Pam Brown next, to ask her a question.

Then on to keep his appointment with Eileen Read.

'This is to be your Home for the Elderly.'

'It was,' Eileen corrected him wistfully. 'I'm not sure I'll get the mortgage now that Philip has gone.' She flicked Bassett a rueful smile. 'Beautiful, isn't it? Used to be a gentleman's residence.'

'Gentleman in the old-fashioned sense, eh?' Bassett gazed at the picturesque country house. 'Too big for me.'

'Too big for most folk,' Eileen Read said with a little laugh. 'Heating costs would be enormous.'

'Is your fireman coming?'

'No, I cancelled. Not much point in worrying about fire regulations.' Her smile slipped. 'I've no heart in it. Let it go,' she said courageously. 'It was a nice dream while it lasted.'

She turned her back. Bassett turned with her. 'I know of a charming little pub where they will be serving coffee and the ultimate in toasted tea-cakes at this hour . . .'

They were on their second cup of coffee when Bassett inquired how long she had known Annette and Olivia.

'I met Olivia when she lived in Dudley—'

'After she married Bertie Mulholland?'

'Shortly before. I was a guest at their wedding. It was one of those friendships which blossom and fade for no particular reason. We seemed always to be bumping into each other in the beginning—when Olivia was with the Samaritans, if I remember correctly. I wasn't married,

Olivia was; I had no steady boyfriend and it's rather awkward saying yes, I'd love to come to dinner, may I bring Jeremy one week, James the next. The friendship faded away . . . Annette I met for the first time a week or so ago. We had spoken on the phone, when I rang up Olivia and Annette answered. I hadn't known Olivia had a sister. Although I don't think I was all that surprised. Olivia had sometimes referred to a Certain Person who had let her down.'

'Annette had let her down? I wonder what she meant by that?' Bassett said mechanically.

'She didn't say.'

'Your friendship with Olivia died and was rekindled,' Bassett conversationally. 'Happens to all of us. We suddenly remember an old friend or school chum and begin to wonder where they are now.'

'In my case it was my marriage. I put Olivia on the guest list, she didn't reply to the invitation and I didn't learn until too late that she had moved to Scotland to live. I sent her a card.'

'And now wished you hadn't,' Bassett said, perceiving her regret.

A half nod. 'I'd forgotten all about it. Her phone call came out of the blue two months ago. She wanted my advice, she said; she was living in a new area and there was no one else she could turn to. She told me about the Meddlars. I advised her to go and talk to them; as long as they were happy all she could do was make suggestions. A fortnight went by and she phoned me again. And again. And again,' she said wearily.

In a different voice, 'I should have obeyed my instincts and told her very firmly, No. Instead I went to tea, brought her some snapshots, told her of my "gentleman's residence" and offered her a job.'

'You did *offer* Olivia a job, then,' Bassett said.

'Yes . . .'

'I hear doubt.'

'I changed my mind, Mr Bassett.'

'When did you tell her?'

'Yesterday. I took a coward's way out. I told her that there would be no retirement home now.'

'How did she take it?'

'Not very well,' Eileen Read said. 'If it's cash I'm going to be short of she has money to put into the venture. I couldn't accept, of course.'

'You couldn't accept because you had already changed your mind about the job. May I hazard a guess as to why you changed your mind? If you ladies are at all like my dear late wife you would have *exchanged* snapshots. You brought snaps of you and Philip—and Olivia gave you snaps of her and Annette. You showed them to your husband, and he recognized . . . ?'

He didn't finish. Eileen Read finished for him.

'Did you ever, at any time, Mrs Read, tell Olivia or Annette that Philip would see the Meddlars?'

'No.'

'Did you ever discuss Philip's work?'

'No, I'm sure I didn't.'

They talked for a while longer.

Eileen Read supplied what Bassett had been short of— the true motive for her husband's murder.

Back at home Bassett made two telephone calls, one to Dabs Wilson to tell him he would be leaving an envelope marked urgent on his desk for Monday morning, a second to the Calor Gas delivery man, whose name was Cook.

'Mr Cook! Sorry to trouble you on your rest day. Ex-Detective Chief Superintendent Bassett here. I'm working with Inspector Greenaway on the Cooper's Lane murder inquiry. You saw the Datsun involved in the case on the morning of Saturday the 17th. Also a blue Ford Fiesta. Did you see any other vehicle in Cooper's Lane that morning, moving or stationary? . . . You did, good . . . Yes. Yes, I have that. Yes indeed . . . Excellent. You've been a great help. Thank you.'

He had his murderer: how to prove it?

Bob Greenaway put the same question to himself, Bassett and Andy Miller when the three met up after Sunday lunch.

'Start with police records,' Bassett suggested. 'And keep fingers crossed about those prints I've left for Freddie Wilson.'

After that, for Bassett, it was a matter of waiting.

Bob Greenaway's call came late on Monday afternoon. 'Central Records Office has turned up trumps.'

On Monday evening Bassett accompanied Bob and Andy to the Mulholland/Gray home.

CHAPTER 24

'We have a problem, Mrs Mulholland. One or two inconsist-encies which need clarification.'

They were all in the sitting-room, Annette looking un-ashamedly worried, Olivia self-possessed. Bob was there, Andy taking notes; Bassett was doing the talking.

'You weren't here to be interviewed when we were making routine inquiries; you and I did speak to each other on the telephone, I'm sure you remember. You felt responsible, you said, for Philip Read's death.'

'Still do. If it hadn't been for me poor Philip would never have gone near the Meddlar place.'

Bassett nodded. 'You asked for him to go.'

'No, I asked Eileen.'

'And Philip went in her stead; I see. Now, when we questioned your sister, Mrs Gray—we needed to know where everyone was on the day Mr Read met his death, you understand—she told us about a telephone call which contained a message for you. You went out before she had time to give you the message. I believe she finally got round to telling you at about half past one, by which time sadly, and unbeknowns to all of us, the man had been dead for two or more hours. According to Mrs Gray you were somewhat annoyed. Can you recall what you said to your sister?'

Olivia Mulholland pouted. 'If I was annoyed I could have said anything. No, wait a moment.' She looked at Annette. 'I was annoyed with Eileen. Because she hadn't told *me* Philip was going. She'd gone over my head, you might say.'

'You didn't know.'

'No, I didn't know. If Eileen says I did—'

'Oh, but she doesn't,' Bassett said calmly. 'She and her husband decided between them. But that raises a question in my mind about the conversation you and I had on the telephone. One of the inconsistencies. I gained the distinct impression that you *did* know about Philip Read's intention to visit the Meddlars. You explained why he was the best person to have gone. He had the knowledge and expertise, was wonderful with difficult children, you said, and Robby was a child really, wasn't he. Philip would have been able to assess the situation, make recommendations.'

A frown came and went. 'Well, isn't that why he took it on?'

'But how did you *know*, Mrs Mulholland?'

'Someone must have told me. Eileen. Eileen must have told me about his experience and I put two and two together.'

'It wasn't Eileen. Eileen never discussed Philip's work with you beyond the fact that he held a senior position.'

'I'm sorry, she must have. Where else would I get it from?'

Where indeed? Bassett said to himself.

'We'll move on to the Saturday morning. Saturday the 17th. You were in the kitchen when Annette took a telephone call. She was in the hall, had Mrs Brown with her. Mrs Brown overheard Annette's side of the conversation. It went something like this: "Who? . . . Oh, Philip. Hello . . . Are you in Glevebourne now? . . . You are, where? . . . You're almost there." She then gave directions. After which she said, 'Are you? . . . Cooper's Lane, yes . . . Good luck . . . Yes, please do. I look forward to meeting you.'

'When Mrs Brown saw Annette leave the house not long afterwards she assumed that Annette had gone to meet Philip, whoever he was.'

Here Bassett addressed Annette. 'Where did you go, Mrs Gray?'

'To the shop,' she said hesitantly.

'To the shop for knitting wool,' Bassett said. 'In fact it was you who went to meet Philip Read, Mrs Mulholland. You heard the name, "Philip", you heard "Glevebourne". Philip was in Glevebourne. "Are you? Cooper's Lane"—must mean, could only mean, you told yourself, the Meddlars. My God! he was going to see the Meddlars! "Look forward to meeting you"— he was coming here afterwards!

'You couldn't have that. He had to be stopped. Didn't he?'

No reply, Bassett continued slowly. 'You left the house ostensibly to change your library books. You parked your car high up in Cooper's Lane, in the only other lay-by there was, and you walked via the lower slope of the hill to the foot of the Meddlar track. Waited until you saw the Datsun coming. Perhaps you waved him in to the lay-by . . . I got your message, you would have said. Eileen has sent you, has she? . . . *That* was when you heard about Philip's knowledge and experience. He would have explained his being there, true or not. He told you Eileen thought he would make a better job of it than either of you, and why. You went with him up the track, where you hit him—'

'Where Mrs Meddlar or Robby might have seen me? Ridiculous!'

Bassett shook his head. 'You didn't care if they saw you. You were prepared to take the risk. If they saw you, so what? Who would believe a madwoman and her simpleton son? Always supposing they cried murder anyway.

'You guessed the Meddlars might hide the body. It didn't matter to you whether they did or not, but the woods were Robby's territory, there was every possibility that he would put the body where it might never be found. You therefore made sure of leaving the murder weapon in a strategic position. Leave it with the body, there was every chance it would be cut up and burnt; toss it in the woodshed, same end. So you threw it into undergrowth at the top of the track. You knew that regardless of what the

Meddlars did with the body, once he was found to be missing the police would search the entire lay-by area. You made sure they would find the murder weapon— where it would do you the most good: it would inevitably point to the Meddlars ... Would you like to make a statement now, Mrs Mulholland?'

'A statement? Whatever for?' She looked at Bob Greenaway. 'This is all supposition. And quite ridiculous, you know.'

'You stole the doll, Mrs Mulholland,' Bob said grimly.

'What doll? I never saw any doll!'

'The doll in the photograph I showed you,' Bassett reminded her. 'The doll Mrs Read told you about. You took it from the Datsun after you killed Philip Read. You couldn't help yourself. You couldn't resist it, could you? Couldn't resist stealing it?'

'Annette! Tell them. Tell them I didn't steal the doll. *Tell them!* . . . No, you won't will you? You never would. You'd let them walk all over you sooner than stick up for me. Wouldn't you? Let them walk all over you . . .'

'While you were on the hillside making your way to Tree Tops, the Meddlar home,' Bassett continued when she had quietened, 'you had seen Dr Hyde's car leaving Boon Farm. You realized that when he got to the second lay-by he would have seen your car there. You had to think quickly. What excuse could you give for being there—?'

'I was picking wild flowers.'

'Ah. Well, that would have been as good a reason as any,' Bassett said. 'I've no doubt you grabbed a handful for credence. You then drove on to the farm, stopping off, as you thought, for a word with Megan Collier. Megan wasn't at home, her husband was. He told you of Mrs Boon's demise, and you immediately took advantage: you made yourself useful. A perfect cover.

'The next day, after you'd had the doll out of its box, you had the collywobbles. This was not an ordinary doll. It wasn't a mass-produced doll you could have bought from a chain store or market stall, this doll was something special, you didn't dare hang on to it. So you returned to offer your services once more—and you shoved the doll inside one of the black plastic bags standing in the Colliers' lean-to, bags you supposed had been put out for the dustmen.

'Unfortunately for you the bags were there only temporarily, they were destined for the Bring and Buy Sale, and so the doll came to light . . . Is there anything you would like to say now, Mrs Mulholland?'

'You are telling the fairy story, Mr Bassett, not I.'

'Very well, I shall tell you why you killed Mr Read. You are a kleptomaniac. A thief by nature. You have been in court several times. On at least two of these occasions Philip Read was present. You had to kill him to prevent him from coming to your house. You knew he would recognize you—and you knew that when he did your job as manager of Eileen's rest home would be no more. Eileen couldn't in all conscience have employed someone who might pilfer the belongings of her ladies and gentlemen, not to mention other staff.'

'How ridiculous!' Olivia said excitably. 'Eileen is my friend. Philip was her husband—!'

'You didn't know that he was Philip Read, though, did you? When Eileen wrote you a card informing you of her marriage she reminded you of her maiden name, but she signed the card plain "Eileen". She didn't tell you her married name. She subsequently spoke to you on the telephone, after a gap in time during which the euphoria of being Mrs had toned down. You were Eileen and Olivia. If her husband was mentioned at all he was referred to merely as Philip. It wasn't until Eileen paid you a visit and brought some snapshots that you understood.

'When looking through those snapshots it came to you that you had made a terrible mistake. You said as much. Your sister assumed you were thinking about the Meddlars,

were having second thoughts. In reality you realized you
had made a mistake when you got in touch with Eileen; you
shouldn't have done it, you should never have got in touch
with anyone from your past, you should have let sleeping
dogs lie.'

The woman shot to her feet. 'I don't want to listen to
any more of this.' She shook a fist at her sister. 'This is all
your fault, Annette. Don't think I don't know: you had a
high old time laying down the poison behind my back. You
little minx. Coward! You are a coward, Annette.'

Bassett appeared to sympathize. 'Annette let you down
once before, didn't she? When she was a nanny in Birmingham?' He carefully avoided looking at Annette.

Olivia swung round to face him. 'They couldn't prove a
thing. Not a thing,' she said plaintively. 'All sorts of
people—weird characters—had the run of their house, but
she let them sack her.' She sat down heavily. 'She didn't
speak to me for years afterwards. Left me high and dry
after we had become such friends.'

'You did steal from her employers, didn't you? Annette
would have gone quietly in order to protect you. Isn't that
how it was?'

'They had no proof. You have no proof now!' The big
handsome face thrust forward as if to drive a point home.
'I could tell you anything I liked—and it would be your
word against mine.'

Bassett was reading her now. He willed the others to
remain silent, and smiled at her with his eyes. 'Then you
won't mind telling me what you did with your raincoat. Did
you have it cleaned on your way to Scotland?'

'No.' Got you! 'I took it off. I'm not as stupid as some
people think. It was my dress that got spattered. I put my
cardigan back on, and my raincoat. Not a mark on the coat.
Go and see, it's hanging up in the hall. I went to Scotland,
didn't I? Took the dress, cardigan and briefcase with me,
and my shoes, tights, everything I wore that day, and threw

them into a loch. Everything save for the raincoat. The coat is clean, thus proving I didn't kill Philip Read.'

Bassett chuckled. 'Clever, Mrs Mulholland. The doll—you would have wiped that; the face, hands, anywhere you had touched it.'

'Even the hat and little pair of glasses.' Pleased with herself.

'The box? Inside and out?'

'Polished till my fingers ached.'

'The perfect murder,' Bassett said admiringly. 'To go to all that trouble for a doll you thought was going to end up on a refuse dump.'

'Ah, but I watch television. I've seen them searching dumps for clues.'

'Of course. That would be why you didn't dispose of your clothes in the bag with the doll.' Bassett was stalling now, urging the telephone to ring.

It rang. Andy Miller slipped away to answer it.

He returned carrying a parcel half-wrapped in brown paper, and a roll of Sellotape, both of which he gave to Bassett.

'Most murderers make one mistake, Mrs Mulholland,' Bassett said, his voice and manner unaltered. 'You made yours when you applied a fresh strip of Sellotape to the box to hold the lid fast. I was watching someone wrap and seal a parcel the other day. She gripped one end of the Sellotape strip between forefinger and thumb, like this.' He demonstrated. 'And so, I fear, did you.

'You were *so* careful. You re-sealed the box only after you had wiped it and the doll clean. You polished the outside of the box. Polished it until it shone, no doubt. A transparent box that looked like glass. But in spite of all that attention and effort you did leave a fingerprint behind—perfectly preserved between the two surfaces, the surface of the box and the Sellotape. So you see—we do have proof. I'm sorry.'

CHAPTER 25

'You must have known about the fingerprint before you came last evening,' Annette accused quietly.

It was the following day, and Annette had asked Bassett to morning coffee.

'I knew,' Bassett confessed.

'The telephone was timed to ring when it did.'

'More or less. It might have been necessary to spring a surprise.'

'I think you did. Why did you string it out? I'm curious.'

'The fingerprint on its own was not conclusive,' Bassett explained. 'It was not found at scene of crime. The fact that the doll's box had been opened and sealed again proved that it had been somewhere else between the Datsun and the rubbish bag. Olivia could have profited from that. She could have maintained that she found the doll. She could have said that you had it and she disposed of it for your sake. There were any number of explanations she could have given for the doll having passed through her hands.

'I've only just now learnt that Forensics found tiny fibres of wool on the murder weapon, they think from an off-white or fawn-coloured knitted glove. In due course they will identify the wool, et cetera. There are a pair of fawn-coloured knitted gloves on your hall table. Are they yours? Or Olivia's?'

'Mine. I knitted us both a pair.'

'Where are Olivia's? With her clothes and shoes in a Scottish lake? Can you prove that you knitted two pairs? Could you prove that they weren't your gloves Olivia wore on the day of the murder? . . . Do you understand? We had to have the rest.'

'What will happen to her? She's not a *bad* woman.'

Bassett stifled a sigh. The vagaries of human nature. Kills a man, ruins a woman's life, fixes it so that another innocent man will be punished for her crime . . . ! He banished unkind thoughts.

'She's—unstable,' he said. 'Unbalanced. She didn't see that Cissie Beardmore was senile, or if she did she paid no heed, her mind was too firmly fixed on what she saw as her mission. Also, she overlooked the fact that while she recognized Philip Read from the snapshots Eileen gave you both, Philip Read was bound to recognize her from the snaps she gave to Eileen. Which he did. Killing him would not have saved her the job with Eileen. From the moment Eileen showed the snaps to her husband there was no job.'

'Poor Olivia.'

Mad as a hatter, in Bob Greenaway's opinion; flitting round the station congratulating herself for so nearly getting away with it, and them for making sure she didn't.

Yet in a roundabout way she had done Robby a big favour. The man was exceptionally happy where he was, had been on outings with new friends, *wanted* to be adventurous now. His mother would be going into a home, Robby would be able to visit her. And if he ever did come out for good he had a nice little nest-egg to fall back on. His future was rosy.

Bassett mused on; private thoughts. Unbalanced or cunning? He was glad he wasn't judge or jury. He had his own ideas. As Hercule Poirot once said of a murderer: 'Cocky enough for anything.'